JOANNE NUNDY

Run from the Dead: Book 1

A Zombie Apocalypse

First edition

This book was professionally typeset on Reedsy.
Find out more at reedsy.com

Contents

Prologue

Norman made his way over to the buffet tables, eyeing the selection in front of him. The meaty smells of an all-day breakfast filled his nostrils. He piled his plate to the edges so he wouldn't have to return: sausages, bacon, mushrooms, fried eggs, hash browns, and of course, baked beans. Even though it was his evening meal, he couldn't resist a fry up.

He navigated his way to an empty table, trying not to spill anything on his suit, whilst other ferry-goers jostled to the buffet selection. But his hands were shaking too much; bean juice spilt straight down his tie.

He tutted and tried to steady the unusual trembling. He was returning from a business trip in Rotterdam that had proved a complete waste of time. He hated these trips, and in particular, he despised the ferry crossing.

"Oi, wanker!" someone shouted.

Norman looked across the cafeteria; a passenger was waving to get the attention of his mate across the crowded room of diners. This type of behaviour wasn't uncommon on "Dutch dash" ferry trips. It was precisely why Norman was going to insist he wasn't to do these anymore. He was terrible at the deals as it was, and he was sure his colleagues laughed at him behind his back. If he thought about it, they probably sent him on purpose to get his fat arse out of the office. He pondered quitting for the fiftieth time that week.

Norman sighed, finally finding an empty table, and placed his plate onto it, beans sloshing over the sides. The mess only added to the leftover crumbs from a previous occupant. Some lowly paid cleaner would deal with it later, after all the gluttons had fled the dining room.

He pulled the chair out to seat himself in front of his excessive meal and sank down. He missed. Norman's large backside caught the only edge of the seat, sending it spiralling away from him. He plummeted to the floor and grunted as he hit the ground, but his pride was more damaged than any body part.

"Haha! Look at that fatty on the floor," said the man who had yelled across the room a few moments earlier.

Norman now clawed to get himself up. The stinky carpet beneath him sent up disgusting food smells, too, adding to his loathing.

"Oh dear, does he need help?" an old lady commented to her friend.

A father from the next table stepped towards Norman. "Come on, pal, I'll give you a hand."

Norman closed his eyes momentarily, wishing the humiliation away. He needed to accept the help. He assessed the guy in front of him and decided he looked a sturdy chap; otherwise, he might have struggled. His sad life washed over him in the same way it usually did, taunting and reminding him of all the mistakes he had ever made. He clenched his teeth and extended his own hand to put this horror behind him. "Thank you," he muttered with a slight nod.

"No problem, fella."

The father returned to his table just a few feet away, where his three teens were seated. They were glued to their phones and were the only people in the restaurant who hadn't seen Norman fall.

Norman retrieved the chair and seated himself. He regarded the slop in front of him and decided he was no longer hungry. The dizziness that had caused the loss of his dignity was still present. Maybe it was hunger? He didn't care anymore; there was no way he could eat any of it now, not with everyone watching and judging.

He caught the raucous laughter of that horrid guy again. Norman had a flash of ripping the man's throat out with his teeth. The skin breaking as he pierced his flesh, the pulling of it, feeling its elasticity before tearing away a lump of skin. The rage that simmered behind Norman's eyes was unfathomable to him. He couldn't comprehend where it was coming from and why. He could almost taste the coppery blood sliding down his own throat and dribbling off of his chin. But it tasted damn good.

He shuddered and closed his eyes tight. *What on earth was that?* Norman couldn't tolerate this with onlookers around. He readied himself to rise from the chair, taking care to not make a fool of himself again.

Norman made a move to leave but found his feet moving in the wrong direction. His eyes locked on to the guy who had laughed at him. He was the noisiest person in the room so most eyes were on him already. But Norman found himself drawn to the guy. Wanting to get much closer. Wanting to hurt him. To bite him even.

No! What am I doing? Norman blinked several times then shook his head hard. *I need to get out of here.*

He caught sight of the sun shining in through the large windows displaying the ocean before hurrying across the sticky carpet. He needed to get away from these people and the rage that had surfaced within him.

He dodged several more people entering the dining room, all giving him disapproving looks. The food smells followed him down the corridor, wafting up through his nostrils and eliciting a retch from his mouth.

His body demanded to lie down once back in the safety of his quiet cabin. These cabins were not made to swing a cat in, though. For a big bloke like Norman, he had to turn sideways to shuffle around his room.

The evening was still early, with the light of summer shining through the porthole. He washed his sweating face over the tiny bathroom sink and looked at himself in the mirror. His usually pale skin was even greyer, and sweat still poured down his chubby jowls. The whites of his eyes were becoming red and starting to burn.

"Oh, great. I'm coming down with something now?" he said to himself.

Even when he was home, he had no one to share his worries with, so he had become accustomed to speaking to the room.

His skin crawled, and he squirmed, feeling the tightness of his white shirt. He felt the urge to rip the godforsaken thing off. Instead, his shaking fingers unbuttoned the front as well as the cuffs. Then he pulled himself free, relieving his suffering.

His right forearm itched like a bitch, so he rubbed and then grated at it with his fingernails. He examined the area, remembering getting the scratch that seemed to be causing the problem. A homeless man had grabbed him in the street earlier that day. He appeared to be homeless, anyway, being so dishevelled and incoherent.

The man had approached Norman when he was making his way through Rotterdam's streets towards his car. The man grabbed Norman's right forearm in a vice-like grip.

"What the hell are you doing?" said Norman.

"It's gonna get you; it's gonna get us all," whispered the tortured man, just loud enough for Norman to hear.

"What? Get off my arm!"

Before Norman could release himself, the man had scratched Norman's bare forearm, creating a tear in his skin.

Now Norman stood in his cabin, staring at the scratch. The homeless man's words were still ringing in his ears. Another burst of rage penetrated his brain and filled his mind. He envisaged tearing the man's arm from his body, lifting it to his lips, and chomping into his flesh. The wrath and hatred piercing Norman's psyche were too much to bear. He had never before felt such ghoulish sensations or the desire to hurt other people. *But why does it feel so good?*

"It's gonna get you, it's gonna get you, it's gonna get you…"

Taunting voices filled Norman's head—and not that of the homeless man, either. It was akin to an incantation, over and over again.

"It's gonna get you, it's gonna get you…"

Several voices sang the tune. Norman screamed and bawled as his mind struggled to keep hold of reality.

"It's gonna get you…"

He grasped his head until, finally, the voices grew quiet.

Norman, now breathless and wide-eyed, stared at the image reflected back at him in the mirror. He didn't recognise himself; a deranged ghoul stared back. The alarm that filled his brain was screaming at him. He realised that it wasn't a conventional alarm but an inhumane one, one of terror and distress. He had to get help; he was dying, he was sure of it. Panic consumed him and propelled him out of the bathroom, over the short distance to the cabin door, and had him yank it open.

Shirtless and struggling to breathe, he staggered out into the corridor and hit the opposite wall. His whole body screamed at him now, hurting in every way imaginable. He scrambled to regain his composure, straining to see anything other than vast corridors and ugly carpeting in front of him.

Panting, he looked down at his own hands, only seeing pale fuzziness instead of fingers and feeling as if they no longer belonged to him. He tried to shout for help, but a gargled cry escaped instead.

There was a loud noise he was sure wasn't coming from his head this time. *The tannoy!* It must be the tannoy to disembark. Although he couldn't understand a word, it was saying.

He had to find someone to help him. Norman lifted his left leg to take a step. But the leg wouldn't work the way he instructed it to; instead, it unbalanced him, sending him crashing to the dirty and overused carpeting.

* * *

The milky eyes of the demon that inhabited Norman's body now opened, taking in its surroundings. Quicker than Norman had ever moved in his life, the demonic corpse righted itself to a standing position. It had no thoughts or feelings of any kind. There was only need and hunger now; blood and flesh were what it craved and what it must seek out at any cost.

A little girl farther down the corridor noticed *it* as her family was leaving their cabin. "Mummy, look at that man over there. He's not got his top on."

"Oh, don't stare, Lilly. Come on, we've got to get to the reception to get off this bloody ship," replied her mum.

Three men exited their individual cabins in the opposite direction at the same time.

"Bloody hell, he's had a rough night." The obnoxious guy from the dining room stood just a few metres away from the Norman thing, laughing and elbowing his mate.

The monster's head spun to the source of the loudest noise and locked eyes with the man who thought it was funny to laugh at other people. Not that the creature knew the guy was a knobhead; he was just the nearest target for the immeasurable wrath coursing through its veins.

The rowdy guy narrowed his eyes and started to back up towards his cabin door. In the next second, the thing lunged at him, sinking his bared teeth into the guy's neck. The funny man's head slammed back into the door and his face contorted in terror, his arms flinging from side to side.

Blood spurted onto the white walls of the narrow corridor and over the man's companions, trickling down their faces. They stood frozen, watching the horror unfold in front of them. The funny guy's screams became gurgles as blood flooded his airway. One of the men sprinted in the opposite direction, down the never-ending passageway.

The funny man passed out, ejecting bodily fluids such as

urine and faeces and a stench unlike no other. His blood pooled beneath his limp body, gushing from the open wound on his neck.

Then his milky-white eyes flew open.

Chapter 1

Anna lifted Jasper's Batman rucksack from beside the door and rolled her eyes at the toy hastily stuffed in the top that she clearly remembered telling him last night needed to remain at home. She pulled it out and tucked it behind a stack of unread post on the cabinet beside the door, then stuck her hand into the depths of the bag once again, feeling around for what her intuition told her she'd forgotten.

"Oh, bugger..." she muttered to herself. *Socks.* She'd forgotten to put extra socks in both of the kids' bags.

"Come on, kids, we need to get going!" she yelled up the stairs before striding up with her head ducked so as to not smack it on the ceiling; a common occurrence at her five feet nine inches.

At the top, she didn't encounter either of her children, which created a crease in her forehead. She entered the first room she came to, dodging toys strewn about the floor.

"Come on, Jasper, I asked you to be downstairs, and you haven't moved an inch."

Anna had raised her voice above the video game's noise and eyeballed him, hoping to put enough fear in him without continuing the shouting. He was her youngest child at six years old, with dark-brown eyes that looked back at her; identical to those of her ex-partner. Both of their children possessed his colouring and looks, and they were a constant reminder she had to share her kids with another person.

Jasper exaggerated a sigh and put down his controller. "I'm coming now," he said.

Anna collected the socks from Jasper's room, exiting and leaving the door wide open. Four stomps down the corridor and Anna was entering her daughter's room. Morning light streamed in through the large window, illuminating the pink walls and white-painted princess bookshelves filled with books, stuffed toys, and a vast collection of glittery snow globes. Alexandra kept it all extremely tidy. For an eight-year-old, she was always conscientious and deliberate in everything she did.

"Alex, get a move on, we're—"

Anna stopped upon seeing her child lying face down on her bed. Her little shoulders shook with muffled cries. No wonder she hadn't heard her mum shouting up the stairs, through a closed door, and with her small face firmly shoved into a pillow. Anna approached and sat on Alex's bedside.

"Alex? Come on, sweetie."

She lifted her daughter up into a sitting position next to her (she was getting big, so this was no easy feat). Brushing Alex's long, light-brown hair away from her face, Anna wiped away her daughter's tears. The smell of coconut shampoo wafted pleasantly over.

Speaking softly, she asked, "What's going on here?"

"I don't want to go for the full week," sobbed the beautiful eyes of a distraught child.

Anna breathed out, searching for the right words to help

Alex through this. The truth was, she hated it herself. The odd night over at their dad's wasn't so bad; it even allowed her to have a bit of R & R. But four nights and five whole days wasn't exactly filling her with joy, either.

"You always have fun with Daddy when you go, and you can call me as much as you like." Anna cringed. Maybe she shouldn't have said that. Steve wouldn't want the kids calling her every day. He hated his authority being undermined. Anna's brow crunched even more; the beginnings of tension built in her shoulders and forehead.

"Will Daddy let me?" Her daughter looked up. Anna was heartbroken for her.

"Well, you'll need to ask him, but I'm sure it'll be ok once in a while. Just make sure you're good." Anna tickled Alex's tummy playfully, trying for a laugh to lighten the mood.

"I'd rather stay home with you," Alex spoke quietly.

"I know, sweetie, but you'll be fine, I promise. And you'll have so much fun that it'll pass in a flash."

Alex replied quietly, "Okay..."

"Good girl." Anna pat her daughter's knee. "Remember, you're going to grow up to be a tough lady, and it starts with being strong and confident."

This was something that clashed with her maternal instincts, though. Anna tried to encourage her children to be independent and have strong characters which she thought would do them well in their adult years, but pitting good parenting against the need to make her children feel happy and loved always made her feel like crap.

Anna twiddled the locket around her neck that had been passed down from her mum to her. She often played with it when she was anxious. She had tiny photos of her parents in one side and her two children in the other; the people she had lost, her parents, and the people she would do anything for, her children.

Shaking her head, she let her hand drop. *Stop being maudlin, Anna.* She attempted to push the negativity from her mind and focused on the task at hand.

"Come on, we need to get a move on, or you're gonna miss the fun fest at your Daddy's."

"Ok, Mummy." Alex's voice had lightened, which alleviated the tension a little for Anna.

Finally, everyone was downstairs and ready to go. Anna piled the kids' things into her blue Fiat Punto while her children climbed into the back seats. She never usually minded dropping off the kids at their father's, but this time it felt different. She watched them buckle themselves in as what could only be described as a bad feeling snaked its way up her spine.

She took in the street around her, seeing the slight breeze pushing at the tree branches and the sun beating down on the earth. The smell of freshly cut grass came in through the open car window, reminding her of her childhood with her parents. Summer days usually put Anna in a good mood, but something else needled at her today, something she couldn't quite put her finger on.

Stop being silly, she thought as she pulled away from the curb. It must be because they were going for longer this time, and she wouldn't get to see them for a week. Anna reminded herself that her ex-partner is their father and would look after them well. And of course, he would even protect them with his life, should it ever come to it, just as she would.

* * *

Anna passed the baggage to Steve whilst watching the kids throw off their shoes and wander off into the living room.

"How much stuff have you packed? We're not going anywhere, you know. I can wash their clothes," said Steve.

Anna pulled her gaze from the kids to stare at him. "Look, it didn't bother me to pack extra things, and it won't hurt you to have it here. Stop your complaining."

"Whatever."

"Alex was upset this morning about being here for a full week," Anna said quietly. "Thought you'd like to know. Oh, and I mentioned you might let her give me a call if she felt like she needed to."

Steve exhaled, looking away. "Wish you hadn't promised that. It's not your call to make anymore."

"For fuck's sake, Steve, I never stop them from calling you. *And* it wasn't a promise; it was a suggestion. I *did* say it was up to you, but I do need to hear from them; a week is a long time for us all." Anna's hands were becoming more animated as she spoke. She could be much more diplomatic when her buttons weren't being pressed.

"Yeah, fine, whatever! She'll be ok, you know. They both will be. I am their dad, after all."

"I know… I've put plenty of her epilepsy meds in there too. I'm popping to the chemist now to stock up a little," Anna said, trying to calm her tone down.

Steve rolled his eyes. "They won't run out. You don't need to be a one-woman chemist."

"And *you* don't need to trouble yourself with my need to

have everything essential to our children. In fact, you may even be thankful for it one day," replied Anna. "And *you know* it's not something to play around with, so stop being such a dick."

She flashed a pained grin before bellowing her goodbyes for the second time to Jasper and Alex. It seemed they'd settled in just fine after only thirty seconds of being there. Anna hated it when Steve was right.

"Bye, Mummy!" they yelled in unison.

"Bye." Steve smirked back at Anna, shutting the door.

Anna climbed into her car and drove away. She gripped the steering wheel, feeling the leather giving way and her fingernails digging in whilst she drove the mile and a half to the chemist. Steve always knew how to get under her skin. She tried so hard to be neutral, smiling, and friendly, but he could always push her buttons. She put her sunglasses on to stop the sun from pissing her off, too, and switched on the radio to drown out her thoughts.

"Extreme violence is erupting throughout Europe, and now the UK with unknown origins. Early reports suggest an illness or virus, and the people carrying out the attacks appear frenzied in their nature. Many sources have speculated—"

"Ugh, that's the last thing I need to hear right now." She switched the radio off and began massaging one of her temples.

Anna then pulled into the chemist car park, shaking her head. She needed to rid herself of Steve's encounter, so she took a moment to compose herself. She looked around and tried thinking calm thoughts. An old lady was taking a lifetime to shuffle across the large space. A mum was pushing a screaming child in a pram, and a man was arguing with a woman, probably his wife. Everywhere she looked, there seemed to be things to irritate her.

Next, she needed to ready herself for another potential argument. The pharmacy had begun to struggle with supplying Alex's medication but Anna prayed this wouldn't be the case today. She locked the car and strode towards the door of the chemist.

"What do you mean there's a supply chain problem? This isn't good enough. Suppose my daughter goes without her medication. There's no telling how bad it could be for her," said Anna, her speech getting faster by the second.

"I'm very sorry about this, madam, but there's nothing I can do. They just cannot get the lorries out of Manchester right now. There're too many delays with the distribution centres. It's been causing a backlog for a few weeks now, and the eruptions of violence yesterday and today aren't helping either. I have three weeks' worth here for you, and hopefully, we'll have some more in by then. But in the mean—"

Anna cut him off with her hand. "Never mind. I'll take what I can and come back next week for an update."

She snatched the meds from the kind pharmacist, but looking at his face made her feel terrible. She usually wouldn't hurt a fly or ever be rude to anyone, but she could turn at the prospect of something hurting her children.

"Look." Anna closed her eyes. "I'm sorry. Not your fault, I know."

She thundered through the pharmacy, noticing that the man had been correct. The supply chain must be causing problems; there were so many empty shelves. *Fucking unbelievable.* Reaching the door, she flung it back and stomped over to her car with her tears of frustration beginning to roll.

She needed to go home, turn off her phone, shut the curtains, and go back to sleep until she felt better. Her head hurt like a bitch, and she knew the only way through it was sleep. When these monster headaches attacked, all she could do was sleep. At least now, she could do it without feeling guilty or woken up every five minutes for a snack. She would wake up in a new, better world with any luck and not this crappy one full of problems.

Chapter 2

The sound of crumpling metal tore through the air. The car in front had reversed straight into Craig's new front bumper.

"What the hell!" he spoke aloud to the interior of his empty taxi.

He had just arrived at the terminal in Hull to collect passengers who were disembarking the ferry. The tunnel was already connected, and there was a long line of traffic snaking from the collection points. But he never expected to be crashed into whilst stationary.

Craig rubbed his eyes; he did not need this near the end of his extended night shift.

He swung open his car door and followed with his legs. He was a massive guy at six foot three inches, so he had to peel himself out of his vehicle each time. He had hoped to upgrade this car to a larger one in the next month, but Craig knew that was out of the window now. Summers were the worst, too, not having air conditioning in this pile of crap.

The car that had crashed into him crunched into first gear. It propelled itself forwards with an increasing whine from the engine, crashing into that car too. It then reversed again whilst trying to turn the wheel. Craig jumped out of the way, frowning at whoever was behind the wheel. He caught sight of a mad old lady rapidly turning her steering wheel and tutted.

Above the squeals of tyres, something else pierced his thoughts.

Screams!

People were running past him, whilst several cars attempted to turn around. He craned his neck to see what the commotion was, seeing running people; lots of them—crowds, in fact. They were pushing and shoving, and some were even trampled in everyone's haste to flee. Then he saw the blood. It covered many people, with some limping and others falling to the ground.

One guy was clutching his arm with blood gushing down it as he attempted to run. The guy then stumbled and fell just a few feet away. Craig darted straight over to him.

"Are you alright, mate?" Craig knelt next to the man, praying he wouldn't get trampled as the crowd surged on.

"Help me, we've gotta get out of here," begged the bloodied man, his eyes darting around.

"What's going on over there?"

"I've been attacked; someone bit me. I think... I'm... I'm gonna... pass..."

The man flopped to the ground, and his hand fell away from his mangled arm. Craig could see he had been telling the truth. He had a chunk of flesh missing in the shape of a human mouth. Other smaller pieces of skin flapped away from the arm, revealing bone. The blood poured out of him onto the floor. Craig could smell the blood; there was that much of it.

"Oh God..." Craig whispered to himself, moving backwards.

He looked around and decided no help was about, so he ran

to the boot of his taxi. He found what he was looking for: an old t-shirt he could use to stem the bleeding. He reached for the boot lid and looked back at the bloodied guy. But now the man was standing again, his back to Craig.

What the hell?

The man lunged at a small child running by with her mother, knocking her from her feet. It all happened so quickly that Craig could only stare. Then the mum screamed a blood-curdling sound that pierced Craig's very soul.

The injured man bit down onto the little girl's shoulder. Craig snapped into action, replacing the t-shirt for the crowbar in his boot. Clenching it in his large hand, he rushed to the scene. He raised the weapon high above his head and unleashed blow after blow down on the back of the attacker.

Nothing happened. The man never flinched or registered being hit. He felt every strike hit the man's back, but it did nothing to stop him. The little girl continued to cry out, as did her mother. Terrified and distraught cries joined together whilst the man feasted on the small child.

Craig lifted the crowbar to his face, looking down at it in his hand. He shifted nearer to the man and used it to whack the man on the head instead, cracking it open like a melon until there was no more movement. Blood and gore spread out from the open skull, and a red spray covered his clothes. Craig wanted to be sick.

He rolled the man away from the crying child and stepped back, allowing the mother to rush to her. She sobbed and wailed whilst cradling the tiny girl in her arms. Craig looked back over at the man he had killed, feeling bile rising in his throat and tasting the acid. The girl continued her screams for a few more seconds before quietening and becoming still.

Craig looked down at the pair; the mother knelt on the road, cradling her unmoving daughter. All he could see was his own little girl, limp on the tarmac.

Suddenly, the child's eyes sprung open. Milky-white and red-rimmed eyes locked on to the woman holding her. The mother's mouth widened into and O, then she scanned every inch of her child for an explanation as she continued to cry. The girl jolted and bit her sobbing mother on the arm. Her teeth sunk into the soft flesh, releasing the blood and allowing it to flow freely. The woman cried out louder but never pulled her child's teeth from her gaping wound.

Craig's eyes were transfixed, and his head shook from side to side, disbelieving. Masses of people continued to stream past them, barely noticing what had just occurred. They all ran for their own lives, not stopping to help or gawp or even mourn this small child. Craig was barged into once, then twice, but still no one stuck around. *What the hell? Why does no one give a shit?*

Tears streamed down his face. He had never cried in public before, being a man of his size and bulk and northern too. Hell, he had never cried before, period. The child struggled free of her mother's arms, who flopped to the side, then laid back, staring into the perfect blue sky. The girl fixed her eyes on Craig. He knew he was next, that the girl would lunge for him; this was what was spreading out all around him.

Craig dropped the crowbar and his head simultaneously, knowing full well he could never kill a child. Even a monster one like this. He sobbed as her teeth tore into his thigh. He felt the skin being ripped from his leg and thought only of his daughter and everyone else's children out there in the world right now.

20

Craig bled out in no time at all, much quicker than he thought possible. Evil images flashed through his mind, then blackness consumed him.

Chapter 3

onk!
Anna awoke to the loud car horn outside.
Honk. Honk. Hooonnnkkk!

"Oh God, get off the bloody horn, will you," Anna cursed the inconsiderate person outside.

Checking her watch, she frowned; it was 4.45 pm. She had slept through most of the day, and it turned out that the horn honker wasn't so inconsiderate after all. Rubbing her eyes, she peeled back the bedding and switched on the cd player to drown out the infuriating racket. Turning the volume up a little, she headed for the bathroom, her body aching from too heavy a sleep.

Anna felt human again after a fifteen-minute, steamy shower. Having dressed in running gear for an evening jog, she switched off the stereo and replaced it with her iPod before making her way downstairs. She needed the jog to up her endorphins and pull her out of this slump.

She searched the cupboards for a convenient snack before running, fearing she may not make it on an empty stomach. Guzzling the cereal bar made her realise she was famished, so she chose a second one to devour whilst tying the laces on her running trainers. *More bad choices, Anna. You can't even feed yourself properly.*

She knew she would need a good ten minutes to digest the cereal bars before her run, so she went looking for her phone. She powered it up at the same time she switched on the television. She lowered the volume of BBC News as she noticed fifteen missed calls from Steve and ten from her cousin Marcus.

Anna's eyes bulged at her phone. "Holy shit."

She hit the call button to return Steve's calls first and removed her earbuds. Her eyes focused on the TV, which showed random scenes of violence, blood, death, and gore, but none of it registering with Anna. She paced the living room and chewed on a nail, waiting for Steve to answer.

"Where on earth have you been? I've been trying to call you all day!" Steve yelled down the phone.

"I needed to sleep, so I switched off my phone." Anna shrugged even though Steve couldn't see her. "What's going on? Are the kids ok? Has something happened to one of them?" Anna replied, her voice rising.

"The kids are fine. Have you not seen the news?"

A high-pitched screech drowned out her reply. She froze and turned to the hall.

"Did you hear that?" she whispered into the phone.

"Yes, just don't—"

"It was just outside my front door. Just a minute, Steve, I'll be right back."

"No, Anna—!"

Anna dropped her phone onto the sofa. She rushed to the front of the house, where more sounds were infiltrating the heavy door. Checking the peephole, she witnessed two women

23

scrapping on the pavement. *Bloody hell, grow up!*

Grinding her teeth, she stepped straight over the threshold and headed towards the women. Anna narrowed her eyes when she got closer to the fighting. The one on top was growling and writhing about like a mad woman.

"Hey, hey. Calm down, lady! What the hell is this all about?" said Anna.

But before either woman responded to her, crashing had her pivoting her head to view the rest of the street. A man was swinging a cricket bat at a group of five people who were attempting to attack him. Nearby, an elderly woman was dragged from her car by a child and an adult, then bitten by someone crawling along the ground. Two men flew through a front room window, exploding onto the street; glass scattered the pavement around them when they landed hard on the asphalt.

Anna's mouth dropped open, and she returned her attention to the two women on the ground. Teeth were being used, flesh was torn from bones, and blood flooded the gutter. The screams were horrific to Anna's ears; she didn't know where to look or what to do first. The woman on top pulled her head up, mouth full of human tissue.

Anna stood stock still in the middle of the bedlam in her ordinary suburban neighbourhood. Her breaths were coming more ragged now as she scanned the area, pivoting on the spot. Her hands were shaking. Growls resonated in Anna's head as a bloodied teenager crawled towards her. One leg had been mauled and had impaired the kid's ability to walk. He crawled over, making her mouth drop open even wider.

She started shaking her head. "No, no, no, no, no…"

The boy shuffled closer still, and Anna finally found her feet.

She moved her first foot away from him, then the next, her senses coming back to life. She spun away from him towards her door and halted.

Her eyes went wide, and she sucked in a huge breath of air. Something had got between her and her door: a man dressed in only his pyjama bottoms, showing a torso where pieces of intestine poked out of gaping holes. A menacing growl erupted from its throat, sending bloody spittle flying from its mouth. A disgusting smell hit Anna's nose too; the intestines had ruptured.

The horror-show-of-a-man charged at Anna, making her scream: "Whaaa!" She didn't even know what word the scream was meant to be. *I'm dead!*

She closed her eyes tight and clenched her teeth. Her whole body tensed up, in fact, expecting the impact from the grotesque man.

CLUNK.

The sound of something hard striking bone could be heard alongside racing footsteps. Anna opened her eyes when the air around her sped up with loud scuffling noises closed in. A neighbour of hers was standing over the pyjama man. *Is he called Bob? I can't remember. I have no idea who pyjama man is, though.*

Bob carried on whacking pyjama man across the back with his lump of wood. The guy on the ground kept on trying to get up, though, like he wasn't affected by the beating. Anna scrunched up her nose at the sound of wood hitting a person.

She stared on, watching blow after blow strike the naked torso of the psycho guy who had been about to attack her. She shook her head from side to side. *This can't be happening, why isn't he staying down?*

A snarl rang out near her feet. Anna looked down at the same time fingers brushed her ankle. She screamed, yanked her foot away, and ran to her door, past Bob and the guy he was still bashing with his lump of wood. She reached her house and grabbed a hold of the front door to slam it behind her.

"NOOO!" Bob screamed and looked back at Anna.

Bob's hand reached out towards Anna, and his eyes reached out to her soul. The ghoul on the ground that had crawled towards Anna now sunk his teeth into Bob's leg. Pyjama man lunged from the floor, able to stand after the beating had subsided. He pulled at Bob's arm and sunk his teeth in there. Anna moved back towards Bob to help, but stopped in her tracks. Pyjama man now ripped a chunk of flesh from Bob's throat and blood spurted all over the place.

Anna flinched. Her hand flew to her mouth when the sound of Bob's cries heightened. She stepped back inside and slammed the door shut. She twisted the clasp, locking out the horrors, the world, and Bob.

Anna leant against the door with shaky breaths and tears streaming down her cheeks. She stared at the wall opposite for what felt like hours. Eventually, shaking hands reached out for the door curtain and pulled it across, scraping the metal pole.

I just left him out there to die, what's wrong with me? But what could I have done? He was the one who saved me. I would have been useless, anyway.

Anna's terraced house had very few windows to the front of her property, thankfully. It was a weird shaped terrace but currently working in her favour. Only a downstairs loo, the front door, and the upstairs bathroom looked out over the horrifying scene out there. A six-foot fence enclosed the windows on the opposite side of the building.

Anna looked up towards the back of her house; she was exposed that way. She darted from room to room, turning off any lights and drawing all the curtains. More of what was unfolding on the other side of the house could be seen through her bedroom window. She continued her quest to block out the world, lastly closing the curtains in the living room. Remembering her phone, she then collected it from the floor and held it to her ear.

"Anna! Anna, are you there? Please answer me, Anna," Steve pleaded down the phone.

"I'm…" Anna cleared her throat. "I'm here… I'm ok."

"Oh, thank God. Did you get bitten or scratched at all?" said Steve, his voice higher than Anna had ever heard it.

"What? I-I'm not sure, why? Look, something awful has just happened, and I don't even know how or what to tell you. Did you hear any of it?" Anna was panting, struggling to keep control of herself. The sound of her breathing was nearly drowning out Steve's baritone.

"Anna, calm down. I have a good idea of what just happened because it's happening everywhere. They are the dead. If people get bitten or scratched by an infected person, they die and return as those things. They attack to eat other people," Steve explained.

"Holy shit, so Bob was going to die, anyway?"

"Who is Bob?"

"He just saved me out there. He's a neighbour from a few doors away. You know the guy in his fifties who is always outside, cleaning his car. Who *was*…" She shook her head to banish the image from her memory. "He got bitten, so he would have changed, right?" asked Anna.

Stop trying to justify the awful thing you just did. Anna closed her eyes at her own thoughts. *I was scared.*

"Yeah, I know who you mean. And yes, he absolutely would have turned."

"Steve, I just left him out there. I feel awful. I just ran to get away from it all, even though he saved me."

"Don't feel bad for that, Anna. You were in shock and did the only thing that came to mind. I've seen loads of people out there freeze up. Do you want your kids to be without you?"

"No, of course not." *I cannot freeze up like that again. I mustn't. I won't.*

"Where're the police? What are they doing about it all?" asked Anna.

"Police? *The army* has overrun all the major cities. It's not just the UK, either. It's happening all over Europe, and there's talk of signs of it on other continents too. Maybe they can get control of it, and let's face it, it's only been about eight hours of chaos, but today has been a total shit storm."

Anna slumped to the floor in the very spot she'd been standing. Running her fingers through her shoulder-length hair, she exhaled a slow breath, replaying the events of just a few minutes ago. The dead were rising. People were dying after being bitten or scratched by the infected—blood lust.

"They're dead."

"Yes, Anna, they really are dead."

"Wow, just WOW…" Anna's brain snapped into gear and she asked, "Where are the kids?"

"Upstairs playing. I stressed that they must be quiet. I don't think my PVC door would stand much of a battering if they knew we were in here."

"Oh God, please don't say that. Keep our kids safe, Steve.

Whatever it takes."

"You don't even need to say that to me." Steve's voice had taken on an irritated tone, then relaxed slightly again. "But yeah, I will. Let's get through tonight; then we'll see what the morning brings? I'm going to stay awake and watch the street."

"Yeah, ok. Can I talk to the kids, please?"

"Yeah, sure."

Anna took a moment to calm her voice before talking to her children. The last thing she wanted to do was panic them. Slow breath in through the nose, and a slow breath out through the mouth. In, out, in, out.

"Mummy!" Both Alex and Jasper were on speakerphone and called out to Anna in unison.

"Hello kids, are you having fun?" Anna was surprisingly good at faking happiness, which was something leftover from her marriage with their father.

"Yeah, we're playing a game in our room with the curtains closed; Daddy said it would be more fun. And that we had to be super quiet." Alex was a clever girl. Too clever really, and Anna knew she would be questioning her daddy sooner or later.

"That's an excellent idea. Listen to Daddy, please, kids, it's very important right now."

"We will, Mummy," Jasper said.

"Excellent, fantastic, wonderful kids. I love you both so much."

"Love you too, Mummy," said Alex.

"Love you, Mummy," was Jasper's reply.

Steve was back on the phone and sounded like he was going down the stairs once again. "Ok, I'll call you in the morning… or if things get worse, I guess."

"Ok," replied Anna with a long, low sigh.

"It might be a good idea to find some sort of weapon. Do you have any bats, or a hammer, or something else heavy to swing?"

"Well, they're not going to get in here, are they?" Anna asked.

"It's a possibility, I guess. Who the hell knows?" replied Steve.

Anna couldn't bear this. The screams and breaking glass were still filtering through from outside. Shaking her head and blowing out a breath, she said, "I'm not sure, but I'll have a look. I think most of my heavier stuff is outside in the shed. I don't fancy going into the back garden right now."

"Yeah, that's probably not a good idea. I'm pretty certain these things are drawn by noise. It's hard to kill them, too, judging by the TV reports. I've seen the army firing bullets into loads of these things only for a few to fall," Steve said. "Just stay indoors and stay quiet, ok?"

"Yeah." Anna went quiet for a few moments before saying, "Keep our children safe, Steve."

"You know I will," he replied before hanging up.

Anna flung the phone onto the floor and buried her head in her hands. She had to return Marcus's phone calls too but needed a few minutes first. Her shaking hand found the locket still hanging around her neck and caressed it, wishing for the ability to touch her children instead. Futile thoughts, but she couldn't help it. Feeling sick to her stomach, Anna raised her body off the floor and headed for the kitchen. She didn't want to eat but knew she needed strength in case of God only knows what.

After returning to the living room, she retrieved her phone from the floor and phoned her cousin back. Anna prayed that

Marcus was fine whilst the line kept on ringing and ringing. But every ring that passed allowed a more profound sense of dread to fill her.

"Shit! Come on, Marcus, answer the phone."

Still nothing. Anna sat back on the sofa, filling her face with all the junk she wouldn't usually allow her body to have. She looked around the darkened living room, smelling her favourite coconut candle scent and seeing the flickering images on the tv. *What the hell has caused all of this?*

She tried not to think of her children again, but it was useless; the enormity of the situation sank in.

Chapter 4

Anna wouldn't attempt to sleep that night, either. She had already had an extra seven hours, thanks to the heavy head she had returned home with. Not to mention the lack of sleep from the previous night. When one of those headaches struck, she knew the only way to fix it was to sleep it off. Not always possible with young children around, but certainly possible this time.

I wish I hadn't slept, though. If I'd been awake when all the terror started, I might have been able to make it back to my children. Now, who knows?

Anna picked up her phone again, checking for anything from Marcus, but still nothing. Her fingerprints smudged the screen in the same places.

Anna and Marcus were more like brother and sister after Anna's parents died when she was just fourteen. Marcus's Mum, her Aunt Judy, had taken her in and cared for her like Anna was her own daughter. Judy had lost her sister, and Anna had lost her world. They needed each other.

Anna raised her hands to her face in an almost praying pose, with her fingertips resting just beneath her nose. She kept her eyes closed, allowing slow breaths to keep her from panicking, and paced the room, uselessness washing over her. Shaking her head in disbelief, she stopped walking. This wasn't the person she was; she didn't wait around for things to happen, she made sure she was in control of whatever could happen next. It was her way of stopping the anxiety and panic overwhelming her, and it was something that Steve despised her for, even on their best days.

Anna raised her head from the recently carpeted floor. She needed to prepare; that's what she was good at—recognising dangers and safeguarding against them. Her hands gestured to the sheer incomprehensible nature of zombies, but then her face set and lips pursed. I need to start making plans.

She looked down at her clothes; she was still dressed for running. Perfect for running from the freaks, yes! But not for having to fight them. Then, Anna's eyes widened in horror, taking in the dark red splashes covering part of her right trainer. More of a brown, the closer she looked. They must have happened when Bob was beating the pyjama man. I'm so sorry for leaving you, Bob.

Anna removed the troubling trainer with her mouth curved down at its corners. She used just her forefinger and thumb to pull it off, and with a clatter, threw it into the kitchen bin. After removing the second trainer in a similarly careful manner to the first, she reunited it with its partner amongst the rubbish.

She was a good runner and prided herself on her stamina, but there was a good chance she would be forced to defeat these things hand-to-hand. That's what other people were trying to do out there. A change of clothes was now necessary.

Anna made her way to the wardrobe; the skin-tight Lycra she was wearing was flexible but had no strength to it. So she pulled out thick jeans, a vest, a lightweight long-sleeved t-shirt and her waist-length leather jacket. If she was going to get killed by flesh-eating monsters, she would at least look good doing it. She needed some heavier footwear she could run in too. Perusing her shoe selection, she reached for her trusty Dr Martens.

"Genius things, heavy enough to kick a person's head in. Perfect." Anna gagged and held her hand to her mouth. Knowing what needs to happen and doing it are two completely different things. Anna closed her eyes, recalling the events from outside, then scrunched them even tighter, willing them to leave her again.

She shook her head, returning her thoughts to her boots. She knew she could run in those things; she had spent enough of her youthful years wearing them to find out. Taking Steve's advice, Anna left her jacket at the stairs' foot and searched for weapons. A raid of her toolbox under the kitchen sink only garnered a lightweight hammer. Holding it in her hand, Anna shifted it around to test it and wondered if it would be enough to hold someone back.

She left the kitchen and entered the living room, sighing, then switched the TV back on. She made sure to keep the volume low to avoid alerting anything outside her doors or windows. BBC One was playing similar scenes to that of earlier.

Anna checked her watch and saw it was now 6.30 pm. She had been wallowing for far too long. Worry had gripped her, and who could blame her? But now she needed a plan.

A correspondent from Washington DC talked to the lead presenter, explaining their situation over in the US. It looked devastating. Buildings on fire, people running in every direction, the Army attempting to advance on certain streets only to pull back again upon being overrun. The correspondent was struggling to find words whilst he addressed the BBC from the confines of a vehicle.

"I... I... I am witnessing what can only be described as hell... The gates of hell have opened, and the demons have risen." The correspondent shook his head. "The US Army are trying to keep them at bay, but in all honesty, it doesn't seem to be working. We are at present speeding through the streets to get away from the worst-hit areas, which is Northeast Washington. One can only assume—"

There was a loud crash on the TV, and the pictures went jumpy. There were screams, shouting, and the odd intermittent image flashed up onto the screen until it went black. The presenter jumped in immediately:

"Ok, we seem to have lost our feed. I certainly hope everything is ok over there. Let's recap what we know so far. It appears that this phenomenon is happening all over the world. Reports from Moscow suggest that the rising dead have worse night vision than we do, but are still just as deadly in their ferocious attacks. They have also noticed that shooting the dead in any body part other than the brain does not stop them. A brain injury must occur to halt them from attacking. I repeat, they do not rise again after damaging the brain."

The presenter looked down at his papers, shuffled them, then continued in a level voice, "Well, surely that's good news, we appear to have figured out what we need to do, and it's just a matter of letting the army take it from here. I am currently trapped in the studio, unable to return home as the streets outside are crammed full of those things. We..."

The news report continued, but Anna had seen enough. Steve was right; damaging their heads was the best way forwards. Looking at the tiny hammer in her hand and finding it wanting, she mentally scanned the interior of her house, looking for something heavy-duty.

Suddenly, she jumped from her sitting position and walked over to the understairs cupboard. Yanking open the door, she began pulling out various sports equipment. She found rollerblades, a badminton racquet, and way too many footballs. Unfortunately, none of this was what she was looking for.

"Where In the hell is that cricket bat?" she mumbled to herself, sitting back on her haunches.

Then it dawned on her the last time they had used it; Jasper had covered it in mud from throwing it into a very muddy puddle. It now resided in the shed in the garden. "Shit!" Anna clenched her fists, wishing she had got around to cleaning the stupid thing. It wasn't a full-sized cricket bat but could do the job much better than that tiny hammer and hopefully wouldn't slow her down too much on the journey to Steve's. Wow, the journey to Steve's! She closed her eyes against the rising sick feeling.

Anna stood up and placed her hands on her hips, pushing the thoughts away. She began tapping her foot, looking towards the covered windows that overlooked the garden and beyond. A pained expression crossed her face whilst she pondered how much she needed that cricket bat and if it might cause her more trouble in the process.

She was sure they couldn't see her with her six-foot fence; it was being heard that was the problem. Her doors weren't the quietest, so trying to go out there would be a massive risk. She began chewing her fingernails, indecision weighing heavy. Anna glanced at the TV screen, but that only seemed to have her flinching away. Her eyes landed on the TV mantle and took in the smiling faces of her children in their school uniforms.

A smile spread across her face and tears formed in her eyes whilst she caressed the frames. Replacing the photos, Anna strode from the room and bound up the stairs. She walked carefully towards the curtains in her daughter's room, making sure not to jostle them with a fast approach. It would allow her the most unobstructed view of the street. She breathed in her daughter's bedroom smells and tried to concentrate on the outside world instead.

Anna inched the edge of the curtain material to the side and peered out at the street below. She held her breath, surveying the carnage. Bodies were lying in the street, covered in blood and gore; zombies were feeding on some already dead and some still screaming. Anna's eyes darted left, following a man running towards a car. She leant forward when the man managed to reach his vehicle.

"Come on; you can do it," she whispered.

As the car spluttered to life, Anna clenched the curtain, feeling her whole body tense with her hand. Four zombies hit the vehicle at the same time. Two were hammering at the driver's side, one at the back, and another had managed to get itself on the bonnet. The man gunned the accelerator, and a fraction of a second before he could move off, a massive group of the things shot to the front of the vehicle.

"No!" Anna squeaked quietly. She couldn't tear her eyes from the man's plight, knowing full well he was about to fail. There were just too many of them. Three or four zombies went under the car with squelching banging noises as he attempted to drive away. Anna craned her head to see better, but the vehicle could no longer move forwards. The bodies had stopped it.

Anna felt rather than heard the breaking glass. Her skin trembled, and she began to murmur over and over again, "No, no, no, no, no, no." Eyes wide open, she witnessed a hand disappearing into the broken window of the driver's side. The chorus of animalistic growls grew in urgency, and another hand shot inside to join the first. Anna stepped away from the window when human screams joined the inhuman ones.

Shivering from head to toe, she went to her room, crawled under the covers, and even though she needed to cry, she failed. Anna curled into the foetal position and closed her eyes against the world.

* * *

Anna jolted at the buzzing of her phone in her lap.

"Anna!"

"Hey, Steve. You all ok?"

"Yeah, no change here. Still a complete nightmare outside. I imagine your street is just the same?"

"Yep." Anna sat up straighter in the chair she had occupied for the last four hours. Still watching and waiting, she continued to stare out at the street. Harsh lines had set on her face, and she rubbed at her eyes for the thousandth time that night.

"I think we're all in this on our own." Steve's voice conveyed what Anna had been feeling herself. The gloomy darkness within her room consolidated the feelings they were sharing. "I don't think housing estates are the safest places to be; there are just too many people."

"Or what used to be people, you mean."

"Yeah, exactly that," Steve agreed. "I've seen those things getting in through the living room window of a neighbour down the street. We really aren't safe here, Anna. I think the best place for the kids is my Mum and Dad's. They're out in the countryside, a fair bit of land, a big sturdy fence surrounding the property. Massive house too. Hell, there's even a well. It's getting there that's the problem. Cars seem a no go. I've witnessed so many people getting it wrong out there. Quiet and on foot is definitely the best way, but it's nearly seven miles. With the kids, it'll take much longer than it should too." Anna could hear Steve blowing out air.

She remained still for a moment, then stood and walked into the next room, taking in the boyish wallpaper and toys scattered on the floor. Picking up a small teddy from the bed, she stroked its fur before holding it to her chest.

"Are you still there?"

"Yeah, I'm here." Anna cleared her throat after hearing her croaky voice.

"We need to leave—and soon," Steve said.

The bear fell to the carpet as Anna's arms flew to the sides and she hissed, "What? On your own? That's insane, Steve. You'll get the kids killed."

"I don't think I have a choice. Didn't you hear me, Anna? They're coming in through the windows, for fucks sake."

"I did hear you, but…" Anna's mind spun a thousand times over, trying to find some way of getting to her children safely. She felt sick at the thought of them outside with those monsters. There was only one solution. *There's no way in hell am I letting them do it without me.*

"Steve, I'm coming too."

"Don't be ridiculous. How on earth can you get here? You'll be dead before you make it to the end of your street."

Standing up taller, Anna clenched her teeth a little. "I *can* do it. Give me until it is dark again to get there. I think night time travel is the safest, anyway; they can't see too well, so travelling with the kids through the night is the better option. Just wait until then, *please.* I beg you."

A few moments passed. Anna could imagine Steve running his hand through his greying hair. She held her breath, waiting for him to agree and desperately hoping he would.

"It sounds like madness, Anna, but I'll wait until tonight. If you're not here by then, we'll have to leave without you."

Anna blew out the breath she had been holding and said, "I will get there, Steve, trust me. I'll do whatever it takes."

Anna hung up. She was now sitting on Alex's bed, touching her daughter's furry scatter cushions. She then reached for her locket once again and closed her eyes against the pain. Withdrawing her hands, she squeezed both of her fists, creating crescent indents on her palms.

"I will get to my kids; I'll run all the way if I have to."

Chapter 5

"What do we do now? Rob! What are we gonna *do?*" said Jack.

Rob was ignoring his brother the best he could, not wanting to answer his questions just yet. Jack touched his arm, making Rob jerk his head round to face him.

"What?" Rob was shaking his head, but as much as Jack could get on his nerves, he did love that boy. At fifteen, he still seemed too childish to be anything other than a son to him. At only eleven years older, Rob couldn't actually have been Jack's father, but he had seen far more than most his age.

"What. Are. We. Going. To. Do?" Jack emphasising his words always set Rob's teeth on edge.

"Cocky little shit!" Rob went back to the window he had been staring out of for the last hour.

"Oh God," said Jack. Rob could almost hear him rolling his eyes.

"Look, I don't know, alright? I'm trying to suss it all out; the best way forwards is always to have as much information as possible. There's no way you ever want to step into an unknown situation." Rob's army training was so ingrained he didn't think he could ever leave it behind him.

It was just the two of them now after their mum had passed

away three months ago. Jack had never had to feel the level of responsibility that Rob had; his whole life, he had been looking out for others.

First, his mum, who couldn't identify a bad boyfriend until *he* finally left *her*. With a single Mum who was pregnant with another son, Rob stood up as the man of the house at eleven years old. He looked after his mum and little brother until she managed to get it all together and be the mum Jack needed. Rob then joined the Army at nineteen, which turned him into the man he was today.

"It says on the TV that you can kill 'em by damaging their brain." Jack fidgeted, looking through the same window Rob was.

"The best way to stay alive is by staying away from them. Do not go out there. Are you listening to me, Jack? No matter what." At those last words, Rob moved Jack to face him and stared him square in the eyes.

Jack hesitated, then nodded back to Rob. Frowning, Jack looked back through the window. Rob eyed his little brother whilst standing by his side, noticing for the first time how tall he had become, almost matching his six feet.

Rob rested his hand on his brother's shoulder. "I just don't want anything to happen to you, Jack. It's too messed up out there right now. Waiting is the best option—at least until we know more."

"Yeah, it is messed up."

"Come on, let's get a bit of sleep, and we can assess better in the morning." Rob led Jack away from the window, trying to shield him from the world's worst atrocities, just like always.

***

Anna needed to get that bat, and she needed to get it now. She formulated a plan in her head. First, pack a bag. Second, get that bat and head straight out into the world before she could draw any of those things to the garden. The last thing she wanted was to be surrounded by them, trapped in her own house.

Anna put three things into a backpack, then took two straight back out. Indecision was crippling her. She blew out an angry breath, grabbed three bottles of water from the fridge, lightweight food, most of it being junk, a small sewing kit, a first aid kit, hammer, two huge kitchen knives, scissors, spare socks and underwear, all of Alex's meds, and a roll of gaffer tape. *Gaffer tape is good for everything, right?*

She zipped up the backpack and slipped it on over her leather jacket, then slipped it back off again to remove the hammer. She placed the pack back on her shoulders and adjusted the straps. Then she grabbed a hair tie off the kitchen worktop to tie back her blonde, streaked hair.

Anna went to her daughter's bedroom and edged a small portion of the curtain back. Most of the zombies were down the other end of the street. They had gathered around someone's garden fence. Anna swallowed; it could be her fence they were charging at next.

She blew out a long breath, rotating her joints, stretching out her body and bouncing on the spot, readying herself for what was to come. Her heart was pounding through her chest, and sweat had already started to trickle down her back. She

43

touched her locket with determination, grasping it in her whole hand. *Mummy's coming, kids!*

It wasn't a hot morning just yet; the sun was just beginning to rise. Anna returned to the kitchen and looked around for what may be the final time. Grabbing the shed keys off the hook, she separated the key she needed, not wanting to make any unnecessary sounds out there.

She used her thumbnail to remove the key from the loop but pushed too far, hurting herself and drawing a little blood. It throbbed as she pressed it against her middle finger. *If this hurts, imagine how it'll feel when you get bitten. IF, not when.* Anna mentally face-palmed herself.

Next, she took a can of WD40 and sprayed the back door's hinges, hoping it penetrated enough to reduce any squeaks. She stepped back and tried to be patient, waiting a minute for the spray to take effect. She tapped her fingers against her leg, feeling very separate from her own body. *This is panic starting, Anna. Don't let it creep in.*

She reached her hand for the back door handle but paused, shaking it out instead. She tried again; her right hand gripped the door handle, whilst her left hand twisted the clasp. She depressed the handle, daring not to breathe and white-knuckling it until she felt the mechanism release. *I can do this.*

She grabbed the small hammer once again and eased open the door. Her heart jumped up into her throat; she was sure they would hear it beating so hard. She pulled the door all the way open and poked her head around it. *I will do this.*

Creatures growled in the distance, but hearing them meant they were too close. She stepped out into the lightening morning and took in the wooded area across the road from her house. The darkness amongst the trees called to her, telling her there would be safety amongst the branches and leaves. *I bloody hope so.*

She eased her door closed with the quietest of clicks, but didn't dare lock it behind her. Too risky to be faffing with keys right now. She crossed the grass, heading towards the shed and the cricket bat she needed. *Please, God, do not let it be under a load of crap.* Anna reached for the shed door, steadying her hand and inserting the key. *Please, please, please.*

A controlled turn of the lock and the door was open. Anna stopped and listened to shuffling just outside the gate. Holding her breath, she closed her eyes to steady her nerves once again. She counted to sixty, hoping it would be enough time for the zombie to shuffle away. She then opened her eyes, allowing her gaze to enter the shed. There it was, right at the front where she had deposited it only a couple of weeks earlier. *Yes!*

Anna slid the slender hammer's shaft through her belt loop and grasped the cricket bat's handle. Holding the bat in two hands, she stalked to the gate where she held her breath once more, determining when to act. Her hand inched out to open the gate latch. Her face contorted as she allowed it to open just a crack.

Her eyes felt strange, and she wondered at the reality of everything she was seeing right now. There was nothing to the right that she could see. The zombies were much farther down the road from what she had seen earlier. Anna swallowed, feeling the dryness there. *Where the hell did that zombie go?*

Anna felt the coolness of the gate latch under her fingers, not wanting to let it go. She registered a bird chirping in the distance and then a slight rustle of the wind through the trees to her left. She breathed in and out, looking over to the woods, then pulled the gate open enough to look to the left.

She could see the corner of her fence and the road beyond, leading the way she was heading. A quick right then left with her head, and she stepped out and to the left, into the new world of zombies.

All of her breath left her body in one go. "Fuuuccckkk…" It came out barely audible, more of a sound than a word. The thing was running straight at her. The world slowed down, and the monster took one step, then two. Every muscle in Anna's face clenched, and the feeling travelled down to the rest of her body. She sucked in a lungful of air, then closed the distance on the beast with her own hurried steps. Raising the bat above her right shoulder, she poured all of her fury into that one swing and let it fly, timing it well but hitting its body and not its head.

She smacked it hard, and it flew into the fence with a loud, crunching sound. *Too loud, too loud.* Anna didn't stop to see what had happened; instead, she faced forward and opened up her stride, looking over at the woods. Every step that hit the pavement thudded through her whole body.

She left the path and hit the road, checking left then right, not for cars now, but for the demons that wished to consume her. Anna's legs stretched out into a rhythm, the energy coursing through her veins. Reaching the other side of the road in four strides, she mounted the far path and headed towards a four foot metal fence that enclosed the woods.

Eyes ahead now, she threw the bat over the fence, placed her hands on top and launched both of her feet over it. Her legs were strong as she hit the ground. She reached down for the bat with her momentum carrying her forwards. Her eyes darted about before she headed for the cover of the woods.

A sound came from behind her, resonating through her body. She reached the first of the trees, slowing a little and dared to look back. The old lady had just hit the fence, but could go no farther. *They can't climb!* She also wasn't tall enough to push her upper body over it. But there were two more heading towards it who could.

Anna twisted her head back in the direction she needed to go, through the woods and towards her children. She usually never ran through areas littered with tripping hazards like this. Still, needs must, and she needed to remain hidden from the zombies if she was to make it out alive.

The smell of the foliage drifted up, and flies whizzed past her face as she darted through the dense undergrowth. Anna dodged and weaved, slowing her pace just a little. A fall with a damaged ankle would end it all for her, and possibly Jasper and Alex too. Concentrating on every step she took, Anna made it to the rough pathway that snaked through the middle of the small wooded area. She emerged too fast, though.

Anna crashed straight into a zombie, bouncing back away from it and landing with a thud on the loose dirt footpath. The zombie flew back into another of the dead and they toppled like skittles, arms and legs flailing around.

Anna's eyes widened at the cricket bat that had landed the other side of the zombies. She scrambled to get up when one of the dead reached out its grey fingers towards her. She rolled away whilst scrabbling for purchase underfoot, but the zombie locked on to her back pack. Anna was pulled back a tad before she released her bag from her shoulders.

She ran, following the path this time and narrowly escaped the hand of the second zombie stretching out towards her. *Shit, shit, shit. That was too close. And my fucking bat and bag are still back there.*

The other chasing zombies shot out from between the leaves like rats out of a drain. They barely missed her too as she sped past. Her head darted back over her shoulder and then back to the front again. *These woods were a mistake.*

Anna neared the end of the path that led out of the woods, throwing wild glances everywhere at once. She weaved through the gates that closed off the area and hit the grass that surrounded it.

Everything this side looked clear, so she skirted the woods, following the metal green fencing that ringed it. She checked over her shoulder again; the first two dead danced through the exit closely tailed by the other two, all following her lead.

I'm going to run back in at the next gate and grab my stuff, I need it all. Surely it's empty in there now. The sun made Anna squint as she looked for the next entrance. The lower branches tugged at her hair when she whipped past them too close.

A darting look behind again showed the front two dishevelled things running at her. The guy in front had only his underpants on, displaying a plethora of bites and torn flesh. He was the one she had crashed into.

She locked her eyes on to the next gate after turning the corner. *Fuck!* More of the dead noticed her and ran from the side street she was now passing. She dodged between the u shaped gates again and entered the woods.

Nothing up ahead; that's a better start this time. She ran the length of the internal footpath, getting closer to where she dropped her pack and bat. *Just up ahead, I'm sure of it.* The path bent to the right, momentarily shielding her from her pursuers, and there lay her stuff just a few metres up ahead.

Branches snapping filtered through the foliage in front of

her, and flashes of movement flickered between the trunks. Anna dived into the nearest bush, rolled over farther into it, then stilled everything. Her body and her breathing. But there was nothing she could do about her heart rate. *BOOM, BOOM, BOOM*, it thudded in her ears but was drowned out when pounding feet hammered close by her head.

She closed her eyes but couldn't force out the sounds. The snarling beasts were too close. They growled but continued to follow the path. Another set of feet trailed behind, then disappeared just like the first set.

Anna allowed herself to breathe but tried not to let it out too fast. She clutched her arms across her chest, fists rolled into tight balls. She attempted to control the shaking that had taken over her body and which was threatening to shake the bushes covering her. *Just calm the fuck down. You've been a moron, but you can still get out of this.*

Shuffling feet came close by. *They must be the ones from farther up the path.* She wanted to look, but she screwed up her eyes tighter instead and then her face to match. *Just lie still, they'll go away soon.*

Hiding in the bushes hadn't been Anna's plan when she chose to leave her house, but here she had to lie until the coast was clear. *Maybe it's my punishment for not helping Bob. I should have been stronger out there—and way less fucking stupid.* Anna shook her head in small movements but continued to lay still.

I've literally run in circles since I left my house. Steve is right, I can't do this. I'm a liability. How the fuck will I ever survive out here. I'm hiding in a bush, for goodness' sake.

Anna wanted to huff at her own stupidity but stifled it instead. The dead were too close, and she needed to keep it together to get to her children.

***

Soon wasn't quite the case. An hour later, Anna crawled out from under the bush. *Those fucking dead things took an age to piss off. I had way too much time to think; I did not like it.*

Anna whipped her head around before grabbing her pack off the ground, then the cricket bat. She chose the woods as opposed to the footpath and scurried towards where the metal fencing should be.

The leaves and branches parted when she moved them aside. *Too much coverage now. I hope they can't hear me!* Daylight filtered through as she neared the trees' opening that would lead her back out onto the housing estate. The sun pierced the trees and warmed her face as the sweat built up and trickled farther down her temples. On any other day, Anna would relish a good run in the sunshine and loved the smell of freshly cut grass. Happy memories trickled in. *Focus, Anna.*

The fence appeared like a beacon, with every step she took meaning one more step closer to getting out of this hell hole. She jumped the fence after throwing the bat, using both hands to propel herself over it.

The ground moved beneath her. It was slippery with morning dew, and her feet hadn't connected well. Her whole body thudded when she collided with the wet grass. Bottom, back then head all struck the ground with a jarring hit. *Owww!* Damp coldness seeped through her jeans into her skin, and grass touched the side of her face.

The cold ground seeped into her consciousness. *MOVE!* She rolled over onto all fours and reached for the cricket bat just to her left. Before she could stand, the tiny hairs on her skin prickled. Eyes widening, she gripped the bat, stood, and spun in the direction of the alarm that was pouring through her.

A zombie approached—a little girl in a nightie. Then cracking behind forced her chin over her shoulder; three others had just pushed through the tree line beyond the short fence. *I'll have to face the single beast, it's the lesser of the two evils. Oh, fucking hell, if things ever go back to normal, I'll never complain about working in a bank again.*

Anna faced her chosen threat. They would be over the fence any second now. She stiffened her spine, clenched her life support—the cricket bat—and charged towards the single zombie. Heart in her throat and breath held, she dodged the zombie but was nearly caught out by grasping hands. She slipped on the grass again but stayed upright.

Her brain screamed at her: *RUUUNNN!*

Chapter 6

Rob rubbed his dark stubble and returned his gaze to the bedroom window. His burning eyes needed rest, but the world had gone to shit, and he didn't want to look away just yet.

He tried seeing to the top of the street by pushing his face closer to the glass, but fell back and shook his head. *Where the hell are the Armed Forces in all of this?* He glanced towards the muted TV in the other corner of the room, showing the same images as the previous night.

Rob's face was drooping, so he relented and went over to the bed. He lay on top of the covers, still wearing his army issue boots. He only intended to rest from his stance at the window, but his eyes began to close and his face relaxed, even though his arms held fast, crossed over his chest. *It'll be light out there soon and then we can begin to formulate a plan.*

* * *

Anna's lungs were burning, her feet were heavy, and the bat

and backpack weighed her down. The thing strapped to her body was dragging her back towards the gnashing teeth of the monsters chasing her. *Push! Push! Push!* The words surged through her mind, but her body told her just the opposite; *Stop! Stop! Stop! God, this feels like that intensive training course I took at the gym.*

She turned a corner onto the main road skirting her housing estate. On her right were sets of terraced houses, bungalows, and gardens, all concealing the monsters within. To her left was the countryside—or where it began, anyway. The sun was peeking up over the treetops there and a small river lay just the other side of it, so it was a no-go. She needed to follow this ring road out and over a small bridge that would take her onto the next big challenge. Another large housing estate.

More of the dead. I totally should've moved farther into the countryside when I separated from Steve. As much as I love it around here, there has always been too many people for my liking.

Anna ran down the centre of the road, always on the lookout for any dangers in her way. She snuck a look behind, seeing a few more of the dead joining her parade from in between the houses. *What the hell? Where are they all coming from?*

In the next second, a car came up behind her with squealing tyres, managing to dodge the crowd of dead runners. *How have they got in a car without being attacked?*

The vehicle came alongside Anna, and instead of offering her help, they drove off into the distance, chucking out smoke fumes that went up her nose. Anna, in a state of shock, stared at its occupants: four young men in their twenties all stared back at her. *Fucking chavs and lowlife losers. Probably don't have jobs, either. A chance to prove you're worth more than you look, but instead you prove people right.* Anna shook her head, furious, watching the vehicle accelerating away.

A breathless look over her shoulder revealed the dead weren't getting any closer, but they had continued to gain in numbers. She faced forwards once again, scrunching up her eyes against what she had just seen. A gasping, "Shit," escaped her mouth, and the word *understatement* poked its way into her mind.

Anna glanced to her left, seeing a more extensive set of trees and bushes jutting out farther. She narrowed her eyes and realised where she was; a neighbour had recently told her the council had built a new bridge over into the nearby nature reserve. It would take her through a more secluded path than that of the road bridge farther on. *Is this the right place, though?* She didn't normally chat to the neighbours unless they caught her off guard like Bob had a few times. *Yet Bob still helped me!*

Anna screwed up her face, then studied the bushes again. Another glance over her shoulder sent chills down her spine. More had followed, and they weren't slowing. She could feel the beginnings of the burn in her legs and chest. Running for pleasure with music in your ears, she would classify as fun. Running for your life… not so much. This was depleting her energy stores faster than usual, something she hadn't accounted for.

I'm doing it. Anna zipped to her left and prayed to God this was the right move. She entered the tree line and dodged a couple of tightly knit bushes. Thorns scratched at her legs, pulling at the fabric of her jeans whilst she parted their branches. Her eyes searched for the way. The weight of the bat tugged at her mind; then she lifted it to whack any foliage too big to charge through, hitting groups of flowers and sending floral smells up into the air.

She whacked a heavy set of branches to the side and an ice cold sensation ran all over her skin. There was only a fence here. *A fucking massive fence!* She could hear the rustling of branches and snapping of twigs behind her, not to mention the constant groan of the dead things wanting to consume her.

She pushed to the right instead, having to force her way through a dense mass of foliage. They scratched at her face and pulled at her hair as she fought her way through. Deep grooves were gouged into the top of her hands and the sides of her neck.

She emerged through the other side of the bush and headed back towards the road once again. *That could've ended me right there.* She flicked her head back to see what the situation behind her was. None of the dead had emerged yet. *It seems they're having as much trouble as I did.* But then Anna heard them once again, piling out of the other side of the bushes and staying in hot pursuit of their meal.

She pushed on along the road, looking for the turn towards the small bridge. Anna knew exactly where it was, but she didn't know how many of the dead might be there. It was a narrow section that could prove difficult should only a handful be nearby.

The area opened up in front of her. *Shit! There're too many.* Anna's breaths increased and her heart rate went through the roof. She looked behind her once again and shook her head. The only choice was to carry on running straight, past a large roundabout, and in the direction of Kingswood. *There's no way I want to get too close to Kingswood, there're even more houses over there. It's bad enough shopping on a weekend at the retail park without the dead trying to eat you as well.*

Just then, two men appeared between two rows of houses at the other side of the roundabout. Anna's eyes darted over to where they were, and they noticed her at the same time.

"RUN!" she screamed at them.

They both jumped at the scream and frantically checked the area. That was when Anna's entourage appeared from around the roundabout's bushes. They nearly fell over at the sight but gathered themselves enough to turn and flee. Anna couldn't be sure, but she thought some of her chasers had run after the two men instead. *Wrong day to be out for a stroll, guys.*

As soon as she passed the roundabout, she realised she had got the location of the nature reserve wrong; it was just a few metres to the left. *Oh my God, this might be the path through that I need.* She took long strides towards the start of a clearing, praying with every fibre of her being that this would be it.

She entered the clearing, seeing the path opening up in front of her, and tears stung her eyes. Ragged breaths came in and out with relief. Fresh energy pushed its way through her body, blood flowed more easily through her veins, and new hope took hold within her chest.

* * *

Jack had taken up vigil in front of his brother's bedroom window. He had been awake for a while, not hearing anything from Rob's room, so he went to check what the situation was. Rob was sleeping with snores rumbling from his mouth, so Jack took his turn at the window. Standing with his shoulders squared, he was determined not to let his brother down.

Looking up and down the street, Jack could see that it was empty, no zombies milling about whatsoever. He crept from Rob's room into his own on the other side of the house, dodging the creaky floorboards on the landing. There, he snuck a look around the side of the curtain; he could see maybe two or three, but pretty far down the end of the street. He wondered if perhaps they should make a run for it whilst the coast was clear. He lowered his curtain, though, realising Rob wouldn't go for it.

"But where we gonna go, little brother?" Jack copied Rob's voice under his breath and slumped his shoulders.

He was tempted to wake Rob up to ask the question but knew he'd get the response he had given himself. Instead, he returned to Rob's bedroom window, keeping sentry whilst remaining hidden from the outside dangers.

Jack yawned, his stomach growling at the same time. *Breakfast would be good.* He began to turn away from the window when something caught his eye farther down the road. Someone was moving pretty fast in his direction, and a moment later, he could see precisely why. Jack's heart began beating faster; he neared the window, willing his brain to think of some way to help. The woman's blonde ponytail was flailing around as she ran hard away from a hoard of the dead. He could almost hear their growls; there were that many of them.

I've got it! Jack positioned himself inside the curtains to be fully seen from the road and began waving his arms like a mad man. "Come on!" he mouthed, trying to make himself visible. The woman looked up at him. *Yes.* He made a circling action with his arms this time and pointed his hands to the side of his house, trying to direct her to run around it.

He did it three more times in quick succession, then charged from the room, banging his booted feet on the thin carpet. *There's no need for quiet, anymore; Rob will find out what I'm doing in just a minute, no doubt.* He descended the stairs in four strides and hit his back door; with his hands shaking and his heart pounding through his chest, he unlocked it. Rob had left the keys in both of their doors on the chance they may need a quick exit. It worked just perfectly right then.

As soon as he was outside, the weight of the world pressed down on him. The fresh air hit his face, and the outdoor smells filled his senses. Racing towards the gate, the cooler air whistled past his ears. He didn't have time to pause and think of what he was doing. *This woman needs help, and I can do it.* Pride swelled in his chest at the same time the terror of what might be out here slapped him in the brain.

* * *

Anna had cleared the other side of the nature reserve before she knew it, the loose dirt paths turning into rigid pavements. There was no way to lose the things in pursuit within there, it was too wide open, and everything could be seen. She just hoped that their numbers hadn't grown. *How much more of this can I take?* She was tiring, and she knew it. She had to find a way out of this, and damn soon, or her kids would never see her again.

More houses emerged in front of her, and she knew exactly where she was. The rat runs in this area were legendary; if she made a wrong turn at any point, it would cost her, her life. Not to mention the fact that more houses meant more people, and therefore more of the dead. If she hadn't raised her numbers in the last ten minutes, she sure as hell would very soon.

She made a quick decision to stay on the front of the housing estate. Corners could help her lose her shadows, but they could also present her with the unknown. *Just keep going, you'll think of something? Can I run all the way there in one go without being cut off by more of the dead? And if I do, then what? I'll lead them straight to my children. This is not a great plan, Anna.*

Anna shut her eyes against the pain of thinking of her children. The positivity she had been aiming for had been nagged away by her mind. She tried again, even if she didn't feel it. *Just gotta keep on running, Anna. You can do it—push!*

Anna saw movement in a house farther up the street. There was someone in an upstairs window waving their arms around, and it dawned on her they may be her salvation. The arm-waving changed to a circling motion and seemed to be pointing to their left. *Maybe he wants me to go around the other side of his house? Oh God, I hope I haven't got this wrong.*

Anna allowed a small wave of relief to wash over her whilst drawing on any reserves she may have left to push her on what she hoped was the last few steps. She silently begged for this to be real, for it to be the end of this ordeal, and for just a little rest and safety whilst she regained her energy. *Please, help me!*

Anna was just a few paces away from the corner of the house, and although she knew it was a risk to turn the corner so sharply, she hoped it served her better in trying to lose her stalkers. The first turn was complete, and other than a couple of zombie blobs down the other end of the street, there weren't any other zombies. They did see her and begin to charge her way, but she thought, *Hey, come and join the party, what's two more when you've got a hundred behind you.*

She neared the next corner, composed of a six-foot garden fence, and braced herself for the bend. No zombies, but a tall young man, or maybe a teenager, hung out of his gate. Anna darted in past him, no pleasantries required; she just had to get the hell inside so he could close the gate.

Her hero silently shut the gate and raised a finger to his lips. Anna tried to slow and quieten her breathing. She held a hand over her mouth to minimise any possible sounds that may escape. She was lightheaded and needed air, so she released her hand a little. Drawing in the oxygen had Anna's lungs burning, and she repressed the urge to vomit, tasting it in her mouth. She lowered herself onto her haunches and bowed her head, still clinging to the cricket bat.

The pounding of feet travelled across the pavement at the same time growling drifted over the fence. Anna wasn't sure how many there were, but it only took one of those things to end it all. For the moment, she was infinitely safer, even if it was at the mercy of a complete stranger, and possibly a child too.

Anna waited until there was quiet once more and lifted her gaze to meet the boy. He had been watching her; she could feel it. Smiling, she stood and noticed how tall he was, even if his face did give his age away. He returned the smile, giving her a slight nod too. But then he looked over her shoulder, and his whole demeanour changed in a flash to one of being caught out.

Chapter 7

Rob was standing in the doorway with a stone-cold glare on his face and strong arms crossed across a firm chest. *What the hell did he think he was doing?* With a flick of his head, he beckoned his brother inside. He looked directly at Jack, then studied the woman as she rotated to see what his brother had been looking at. A tall, athletic-looking woman, maybe thirty years old, looking like she was about to puke.

Holding a finger up to his lips, he waved his hand at her to enter their house too. Just being in the garden was already putting them at risk, so she may as well come in before she started hurling and drawing those creatures again. *God knows why she was out there in the first place. Only an idiot would put themselves in that situation.*

The woman looked around the garden before looking back towards Rob. He stepped aside, allowing her to enter. Once inside, the door was closed and locked again.

"I'm Jack," Jack extended his hand towards her and beamed a broad smile.

"Anna!" Shaking his hand with her right, she raised her left to her mouth. "The toilet?"

Jacked pointed to the downstairs loo. "Over there."

Anna bolted to the tiny room and managed to get the contents of her stomach inside the toilet. She retched whilst Rob closed the door behind her, allowing him a few moments alone with his brother.

"What the hell are you doing?" He didn't shout even though he needed to. He had to keep his voice down.

Jack widened his eyes, playing innocent. "What are you talking about?"

"You know full well what I'm talking about. You absolute idiot, you could've got yourself killed." Rob's voice remained low, but the pain in it could be felt. There was no way he would lose his little brother, too, after losing his mum just a few months earlier. Rob cleared his throat. "How could you be so stupid?" He was furious, but more than that, he was scared to death of Jack getting hurt. How on earth could he calm the lad's impetuous nature?

"I did what I needed to. She was running away from at least a hundred of them things, and you would've done the same too. I know you would have." Jack pointed a finger towards Rob's chest.

"Why didn't you wake me?"

"There was no time; it happened in a flash. And whether you like it or not, that woman is alive because of me." Jack stood tall, squaring off to his brother.

Sighing, Rob looked around the room. *How can I argue with that?* He examined the young man in front of him and reluctantly nodded his approval. "Well, have you had any breakfast yet?"

"No, I was about to when I saw the woman running down the street."

Anna closed the toilet door with a soft click and headed to where the brothers were standing. Looking from one to the other.

"I'll be going. Thank you for your help; I appreciate it so much," Anna addressed Jack.

"You don't have to go yet; we were just going to get some breakfast," he replied. "Have you had anything this morning?"

"I don't want to impose; you've already been incredibly kind," she said, but her Anna's stomach gave her away at that exact moment.

Rob faced Anna but didn't look her in the eyes. "It might be a good idea to rest for half an hour at least. And refuel, so to speak. I'm sorry I wasn't very welcoming at first. It's just that I was concerned for my brother. Honestly, you are welcome to stay a little while and look for a clear opening out there." As he said this, she visibly relaxed a little. *Why had she been out there?* he thought. She didn't strike him as a silly woman—quite attractive, if he was looking at her in that way.

"Thank you, that's very kind." Anna closed her eyes and rubbed her forehead for a moment. "I suppose I should eat something. If I'm going back out there again, I need to be ready for it."

* * *

Anna, placing her bat against the wall, slipped off her rucksack and followed the brothers into the kitchen, where she was ushered to a rectangular, wooden table. Whilst sitting, she surveyed the room. A pretty kitchen, very orderly, and lots of paraphernalia for cooking. Not at all what she expected a man like Rob to have. Narrowing her eyes a little, she noticed a woman's apron hanging from the back of the door. *Ah, that makes more sense. I wonder where the woman is. She must be Rob's wife, but then this room screams of an older woman, so maybe their mother?*

"So… um, is it just the two of you?" Anna asked with fidgeting hands. She didn't want to push Rob back into his angry status again.

"Yeah, our mum died three months ago." Jack had answered the question but appeared to become sadder as the sentence went on. Rob had his head in the fridge, but she could see his body stiffen.

Anna's face softened to that of a mother. Reaching her hand across the table, she covered Jack's with her own. He had seated himself opposite her and now looked forlorn, head bowed and close to tears.

"I'm so sorry," There was nothing else to say or do. Anna pulled her hand away, and Jack lifted his to swipe at his eyes.

"Bacon sandwich?" Rob pulled his head out of the fridge and gazed at Anna. His eyes were striking, something she never got to see earlier because he had never looked directly at her face. Piecing blue irises bored into hers, and for a moment, she was lost for words. *I shouldn't have been so nosey; I've dredged stuff up for them. I feel bad now.* Her mouth gaped until she finally managed an answer. "Yes, please, that'll be fantastic." *It really would; I'm bloody starving.*

Anna shifted her attention back to Jack, who still looked grief-stricken. "So, how old are you, Jack?"

"Fifteen now, and I'm nearly as big as Rob already." He looked to his brother, seeking an interaction.

"You'll never be as good as me, though." Rob teased back with a forced grin on his face.

"I'm already better than you. Have you ever saved a woman's life?" Jack looked at Anna, and she grinned, watching grief leave and pride enter the boy.

Anna let out a small laugh, "You certainly did," and flashed him a smile that lit up her face. Smiling felt wrong at a time like this, but it was so wonderful too. She looked over to Rob, who matched her enthusiasm. He changed from looking at his brother to looking at her, giving her a slight nod in appreciation. Together they had managed to pull Jack out of his grief, just for a moment or two.

* * *

Bacon sandwiches handed out, they all ploughed into their food. Silence descended over the table whilst they concentrated on their own plates. Rob's eyes flicked over to Anna a few times wanting to ask questions but not sure he wanted to know at the same time. He finished his off by mopping up the brown sauce on the plate with the last bit of bread.

"That was very good, thank you," Anna said, looking less pale than when she had first entered their house.

"No problem, one extra was no bother." He cast his eyes away from her, so he wasn't tempted to get nosey.

"So, how come you ended up out there being chased by the dead things?" Jack asked, chewing and spraying his food at the same time. *Shit, he had to ask, didn't he?*

"Well… my kids are at their dad's just another mile from

65

here. It all kicked off whilst I was sleeping the day away with a bad head and didn't see anything on the news until it was too late. Everything had gone to hell when I woke up." Anna did a slow shake of her head, looking drained and anxious. "I have to get to my children, and we intend to get them somewhere safer than the housing estates around here. There are just too many people, which of course means too many of the dead." Anna rubbed at her eyes and drew her hand down the rest of her face. Rob couldn't help but feel a pang of sorrow for the woman—precisely why he didn't want to know her story.

"By the looks of it, you only just made it here on your own; how on earth do you think you can make it out there with two young children in tow?" Rob sat forward in his seat, asking Anna this question.

"Do you not think I haven't thought this through? There's no other way. I know it probably looks like total madness, but I can't give up on my kids. I will get them to safety no matter the cost." Anna became more animated with every word that left her mouth. Rob could understand every feeling she was having right now. The ache in his chest was a constant reminder of the responsibility he felt for his little brother. He knew he'd lay his life down for him and was witnessing the same in Anna.

"Fair enough," was all Rob could respond, holding her gaze a little longer than he should.

"Where's the place you're going, then?" Jack chimed in.

"Preston! It's my ex-partner's parents' house. It's a big solid house on a large plot of land, fenced in with not many neighbours. An ideal place, in my opinion. Other than an army base, anyway. The only problem is that it's around six miles from my ex's house, but the worst part will be getting us all off the housing estate. Once we're out into the country, we should be safer. I just need to get there before it gets dark, or my ex will leave without me."

Rob narrowed his eyes at that last comment. *That's why she's in such a mad rush to get there.*

"Couldn't you go in a car?" Jack asked.

Rob sucked in air through his teeth. "A car isn't a good idea. I've seen people trying to flee in a car, only to be swamped by them in a second," he said, and Anna nodded her head in agreement. "The only way to use a car effectively would be once you've neared a clearing where there aren't as many of those things about. Either that or a distraction."

Anna sat up taller, listening to Rob's comments. "Now, that's a thought—a distraction! Maybe that could be how I get my kids there." Anna rubbed her face in concentration whilst looking down at the table as if all answers resided there. Rob could see the sheer determination in the woman. Something he had admired in many others when in the Army.

"Rob was in the Army, so he knows lots of stuff that could help get us all out of this crap."

Rob's mouth curved a little at Jack's assessment of him. It was nice to be thought of in that way, even if he had been dishonourably discharged for violence towards a senior officer. Although the guy deserved it, it also meant he got home quicker to his brother. Their mother had just passed, and Jack needed him by his side.

"It's definitely something to think of; thanks for that, Rob." Another appreciative smile spread across Anna's soft face. Rob once more felt the tug of his heartstrings at her plight. *I'm being sucked in here.*

"No problem, just glad we could help." Rob stood from the

table and cleared the plates away.

Chapter 8

"I need to get moving. Is it ok to have a look outside from the upstairs windows and check the coast is clear?" Adrenaline was beginning its journey through Anna's body again. She fiddled with her locket and knew what she needed to do, so she may as well get it over with. *I need to be with my children.* Hopefully, the next mile would be easier than the first. *Please be easier.*

"Yeah, of course, I'll come and look with you. Do you have everything ready?" Rob looked concerned. He had a kind face when he wasn't screwing it up in anger.

"Well, I have everything I came here with. My trusty bat being one of my tools, I did manage to whack a couple of them on the way here with it. Don't think I put them down permanently, though, I was concentrating more on the running part." Anna sighed; what else could she do other than the running? She wasn't a fighting kind of woman and never had been.

Rob looked at her like he had an idea. "Why don't I show you a few things before you take off? It'll only take a few minutes. Might even save your life or your kids." He raised his eyebrows while he posed his question, looking almost hopeful.

"Yeah, sure, that'd be great. Any help I can get would be fantastic. I have until nightfall to get there, and I just texted Steve to tell him I'm halfway, so it seems I have more time than I thought I might." Anna breathed a sigh of relief that she didn't have to go back out there just yet. Anxiety had started to creep into her muscles and stiffened her up. This slight reprieve lightened her mood just a tad. "Can you give me just a minute first, though? I want to try my cousin again. I can't get him to pick up the phone."

She chewed the inside of her lip whilst pulling the phone out of her pocket. She first checked for any messages or missed calls before hitting the call button for Marcus. Anna held it to her ear, staring at the wall in front of her.

Ring...
Ring...
Ring...
Ring...
Ring...

She hung up and looked up towards Rob with tears forming in her eyes.

"I'm sure he'll be ok. Maybe he's dropped his phone somewhere but is totally safe. You've got to hope for the best," said Rob.

Anna nodded and replied in barely a whisper, "Yeah. He's actually more like a brother to me, but technically he's my cousin."

"Oh, really? How so?"

"Well, my parents died when I fourteen and my Aunt Judy, my mum's sister, took me in. They've been my family ever since. We were always close beforehand, but everything changed after the accident."

Rob slowly shook his head. "I'm so sorry, Anna."

Anna snapped her gaze away from the spot on the carpet she had chosen to stare at. "I'm not even sure why I told you all of that."

"Maybe it's my approachability," said Rob, grinning.

Anna laughed, and her eyes widened as she said, "Yeah, right."

"Hey, what's that supposed to mean?" Rob was still smiling.

"Well, the stare you gave me in the garden wasn't the warmest of welcomes I've ever had."

Rob sucked on his teeth. "Uh-huh, is that right? Well, what about the bacon sandwich? That was pretty hospitable."

Anna smirked back at him. "Ok, you have me there. That was pretty fantastic."

"There you go! Come on, I'll show you my moves."

Anna's eye's widened and a grin of her own spread across her face.

"Oh… That's… not what I meant," Rob stuttered. "I meant the fighting stuff, not the… dating stuff."

Anna couldn't help but laugh. The look on Rob's face was so entertaining. Red was flushing up to his cheeks as he spoke. *He's much cuter when he's relaxed.*

"It's ok, I know exactly what you meant. I just couldn't help myself from teasing you."

"Lovely, thanks for that. I'll get you back one day, just you watch."

"Ooh, sounds like a threat," Anna teased.

"Absolutely!"

Rob shook off the embarrassment and took Anna into the living room for a bit more space.

"Nothing too fancy is usually the best way," said Rob.

"You know how to treat the ladies, then." Anna smirked.

71

Rob smiled back, nodding a touché before saying, "I've been watching these things, and I reckon they aren't too steady on their feet. Anyway, you can knock them to the ground, and it gives you a fighting chance to either run away or deal with another one of 'em."

"Sounds good," Anna replied.

"A kind of sweeping kick to the knees is a good one—or any kick, for that matter. Just make sure you're balanced first. Failing that, you could always throw yourself low, heading for their lower legs. You grab one leg on the way down and use your back to push upwards and fling 'em. Only try that if you're confident, though. It has to be quick!"

Rob demonstrated to Anna first, then motioned for her to copy. She practised a few times, wondering about the man showing her. *What was he like in the Army? He seems pretty competent—probably more of a high achiever, actually.*

He moved closer to her to help.

Hmm, I haven't been this close to a man in quite a while. I reckon he's a little younger than me, but there's no harm in looking. Would I have dated a man younger than me during normal times, I wonder? It's not like I've done a lot of dating recently, anyway. Just been me and the kids for a while now—exactly the way I like it.

Anna wanted to do well at this, so she kicked out in the way she might if there was a zombie in front of her. Then she crouched down into a half roll to try out the push-up, which she was confident she could manage—*definitely something to remember.*

"You could always do a high kick to the chest to push them back too. I reckon that would be quite effective. Next, if you've gotta fight, then finish 'em quickly. It seems the only way to kill them is by damaging the brain," said Rob.

"Yes, I've heard that, too," replied Anna.

"The weak points are the eyes, the temples, and up through the bottom of the jaw. It would always be hard to bash through a skull; I wouldn't try it unless you didn't have a choice."

"Well, yesterday I managed…" Anna stopped talking, because she was sure she heard a child's voice. She held up a hand to quieten Rob too. A second later, there it was again: the wails of a small child.

All the air left Anna's body. "A child!" She whispered. It almost sounded like her child. *Jasper!* She spun and headed straight for the door. Rob grabbed her arm, but she shook it off.

"Get the fuck off me!" Anna growled.

Rob released her arm and stepped back, rapidly blinking at her fury. She unlocked the door in a swift motion and threw herself straight into the garden.

* * *

Jack went to follow Anna, having heard everything from just a few feet away.

"Not a chance, Jack," said Rob.

"We can't leave her out there on her own."

"I'm not going to," Rob replied.

Rob grabbed a small hatchet he had placed near the back door. "You stay here! No arguments."

Jack stepped back, holding his hands up in mock surrender as Rob stepped out into the garden. *Crazy arse woman, she's gonna get us all killed... But it's a child!* Even if it wasn't a child, he wasn't sure he wouldn't have followed Anna out, anyway. She needed his help. Rob also hoped that, just maybe, she might need him too. He braced himself for what he was about to face when he ran through the gate towards the sound.

* * *

Anna hit the footpath outside the back gate and pivoted right. She ran three steps before she was out in the open where she could see the child. He was alone in the middle of the road with his little hands covering his face and crying at the top of his lungs. There were two bodies on the ground nearby, not moving, and three blood-hungry beasts were hurtling towards him.

NO! NO! NO! Anna sped towards the little boy but realised she didn't have her cricket bat. She never slowed one iota. The nearest beast reached out its hand towards the child, almost grasping his blond hair as Anna arrived. She never knew what she was going to do until she did it.

She reached the monster, just off to its side, and grabbed out with both of her hands. She grasped the clothes on the back of its upper body, and, running past it, she pulled with all of her might, spinning at the same time and launching the monster away from the child, towards the curb. Her fingers cried out in pain from the weight of the dead thing, but she never stopped moving.

Anna flicked her head around to see the second creature almost on her. She moved forwards whilst crouching low, grabbing one of its legs and heaved upwards, sending it flying over her back and landing near the back end of a car. *Holy shit! That worked.* The beast was heavy, but her strong legs did all the work. Knowing it had touched her back, though, sent a chill down her spine.

The third beast was a moment behind the second and grabbed onto Anna, baring its teeth. Anna stumbled with the surprising weight and aggression of its forward momentum. She fell to the ground with the monster on top, smacking onto the road. Pain shot across her back. The zombie grappled with her, trying to force its face towards her flesh, and its fingers dug into her arms, getting no farther than the leather jacket.

She squirmed, trying to get the thing off. *It's gonna kill me. No, no, no, no. My kids. I don't want to die, not like this.* She could smell blood on its breath as it opened and closed its mouth, longing to devour her, its teeth inches from her face. She pushed at its chest, but it was like her world was now ending too. *This can't be it.*

Crunch! There was a jolt to the monster on top of her. Then it stopped moving before going limp, leaving Anna trying to hold it up still. She could hear her own ragged breaths being forced in and out, but it was like she wasn't breathing at all.

What happened? She looked to the side to see one of the thrown beasts heading for Rob. He swung his hatchet with strength and precision, chopping into its skull. *Oh, Rob happened.*

Rob pulled his hatchet away from the first beast's skull and lashed out his boot into the other creature, sending it back a few feet whilst he twisted round to face it. Rob finished it off, then released his hatchet again. He walked over to where Anna still lay with the beast on top of her. He pulled the dead thing off and reached down, grabbing her hand and yanking her off of the floor.

He had saved her. *He followed me outside and I never even knew. Why would a stranger go to bat for me like that after knowing me such a short time? And after the way I just spoke to him...* She looked at his face and struggled to hear what he was saying as her breathing and mind caught up. Finally, her brain allowed her to understand, lurching her back into the present.

"Anna! Anna!" Rob screamed in her face. Her eyes focussed on him. "There's more coming. Get the boy NOW!"

She looked towards the child, hearing his cries once more. He was standing where she had left him when she fought off two of the monsters. Anna sped over to him and snatched him up into her arms. *He's so tiny, and he's all alone*

There was no point in trying to quieten him yet; the things already knew where they were. She looked over her shoulder to see dozens racing towards them. They must've lingered from chasing her earlier. *Oh shit! It's the rat runs; they couldn't get out the other end of the street.*

She ran back to the garden where the wide-eyed Jack awaited, holding the gate open. Rob followed them and bolted the gate himself, hurrying his brother indoors.

Once they were inside, she set to work, trying to calm the child down on the off chance the dead hadn't seen where they had disappeared to.

"It's ok, honey. Shh, shh… You're safe now; you'll be fine. Shh…"

Anna switched the boy around in her arms, attempting to cradle him. She rocked him, continuing the shushing sounds whilst gazing into his sad little face.

"Fuck! Did you see how many were out there?" Rob said to the room. "Jack, go and get your backpack and your coat. Did you pack everything like I told you to?"

"Yeah," Jack said.

"Good, 'cos, I think we're gonna all have to get out of here ASAP. The dead are at the back gate." Rob glared at Anna.

Anna replied, "I'm so sorry, Rob. There was no way I could leave him out there."

"You just leapt at it without even doing a reccy of the situation. You didn't consider *our* safety." Rob glared at her.

"It's a *child*, Rob. If I had waited, he wouldn't be here right now. I'm *so sorry* that I didn't do your fucking reccy, but I wouldn't change a thing about it." She twisted away from him, not wanting to look at his face anymore right now. *This child needs me, anyway, so he can just go fuck himself.*

Rob exhaled before walking away.

Chapter 9

Anna had quietened the child. She looked down at his tear-streaked face, and her heart broke. She surmised it must have been his parents out there with him—possibly the ones on the ground or maybe the ones running at them. *I hate this, and it's going to be my children out there soon.*

"What's your name, honey?" Anna asked in the softest voice possible.

"Lo… gan," he replied through stuttered breathing.

"Well, hi, Logan. I'm Anna." Anna smiled at the boy, hoping to relax him.

"Hi." It was so quiet, Anna nearly missed it.

"Were your parents outside with you before you started crying?"

Logan nodded his head slowly, looking away from Anna. She reached out her hand and held his, continuing to cuddle him close.

"Would you like to come with me now? I can look after you, and I already have a little boy about your age," Anna spoke gently. She didn't have the time to make him feel comfortable with her.

"Why couldn't my mummy get up off the floor? And why did my daddy try to bite you?" Logan asked.

"Oh, honey, I'm so sorry. It sounds like your mummy and daddy have gone to heaven."

Logan never said another word. He looked at the floor, slowly breathing in and out and looking so tiny that Anna wanted to bawl her eyes out right there and then. Instead, she stroked his hair before walking over to where her backpack and cricket bat were. Rob came down the stairs and pulled Anna to the side, away from Logan. He looked much calmer than he had five minutes earlier.

"Is he ok?" Rob asked.

"The best he can be right now, I think," said Anna. *I'm still annoyed with you, but I'll be polite.*

Neither Rob nor Anna were looking at each other's faces. Rob took a slow breath in, then out, seemingly finding the right words. Then he looked her straight in the eyes.

"Look, I'm sorry for my outburst. Jack is my responsibility, and there's no way in hell I'm gonna let anything happen to him. But you're right. If you hadn't acted right there and then, the kid would've been got. You did a reckless but very brave thing."

He does seem sorry. Anna shook her head. "Not brave, because I didn't think at all. It was a reaction, plain and simple."

Rob gave her a small smile. "Ok." He nodded. "I've had a look out the front window, and it looks ok out there. We need to move now whilst the coast is clear. Are you ready?"

"I am. I think it might be best if I piggyback Logan, so if you or Jack could carry my backpack?"

"Good idea. Let's do it," said Rob.

Anna knelt down in front of Logan, brushing his pale hair

from his face. "We have to go, Logan. I'm going to piggyback you; that'll be fun, won't it?"

Logan nodded but looked so sad at the same time. And who could blame the child? Anna stood Logan on the sofa and encouraged him to climb onto her back. He was a slight boy, so she might be ok running with him. *Hopefully*, she thought.

* * *

They all convened at the front door whilst Rob drew back the curtain. He double-checked his weapons on his belt: he had an eight-inch Army knife, sheathed and strapped to his thigh over black combat trousers; his trusty hatchet was hanging from the opposite side of his belt whilst he carried Anna's cricket bat; and he also wore a leather jacket, zipped up and ready to go. He looked at Jack. *I will protect you, Jack. All of you. No one's going to die on my watch, not today. Never again.*

Jack shouldered a small backpack of his own, as well as Anna's. Rob had set up Jack with a large knife and a hatchet, wearing the same black combats and thick jacket to finish off his outfit. Rob looked him up and down, checking his brother was ready to go. If anything, Jack looked more gung-ho than both him and Anna combined.

"Ready?" Rob asked.

"Yep," replied Jack.

Anna nodded but looked a little green around the gills. She was playing with her necklace. He wondered if she could cope with being out there again, but then he remembered her reasons for having to. It seemed that any time something to do with children arose, she instantly stepped up, regardless of her fear. He respected the hell out of that, even though he had been furious with her when they saved Logan. *She's got a good heart.*

"Logan, buddy, do you think you can keep quiet? No noise at all?" Rob asked the boy perched on Anna's back. Logan nodded his reply, looking more lost than Rob had ever seen anyone. "Let's do this."

An intensity filled Rob's body from his toes to the top of his head. It was vibrating through him, and if he thought it was possible, he'd be certain his eyes were lit up like fireworks too. The adrenaline had hit him, and he felt ready for anything. Just the way it used to be in the army.

He clasped the door handle and turned the key in the lock. It gave a little release sound that had him cringing inside, but he pulled the door open anyway. The coast had been clear several minutes ago now, so time was of the essence.

Rob pulled it wide open and stepped outside; turning back to address the others, he said, "Stay close."

Anna, then Jack, followed him out into the open. They all flung their heads around, trying to assess the street. Jack pulled the door closed behind him with a quiet click, and they all headed out of the front garden, between the high hedges they had there. Rob led them to the left and halted before they reached the property line. *Jesus, it's like riding a bike. My army training just kicks right in. Along with all the shit memories too.* He peered round to view the street beyond.

He could see at least six or seven zombies down the side of their back fence; the rest must have been nearer the gate. Their growls and thudding against the fence drifted over to the group's location. *They're going to be drawing even more soon enough. We need to get away from here.*

"Right, when I say go, we jog across the street. Keep an eye out left and right. If any start running at us, let me know," said Rob.

Rob checked back around the corner; all the dead were clawing and pushing at the fence.

"Go."

They all jogged across the street, Rob out in the lead, Anna and Logan next, then Jack bringing up the rear. They reached the other side of the road without the crowd seeing them. *Step one complete.*

They continued forwards down the main road, clinging to the garden fences and hedges that formed perimeters. Rob glanced back towards Anna, seeing Logan with his face nestled into her shoulder. *Hopefully he won't have to witness much more horror today.*

They continued along the block of houses until the entrance to the next street emerged. Rob held up his hand to signal everyone to stop where they were whilst he took a peek around the corner once again, his eyes wide open and taking everything in. He first looked across the street to his right, then checked behind them all before tilting his head around the corner and regarding the road they had to cross.

There was a massive crowd of them nearer the bottom, banging on a fence there. The wood was wavering and looked ready to cave in at any moment. This street seemed relatively safe to cross right now, with some poor unfortunates about to become dinner. Rob didn't feel great capitalising on someone else's bad day, but he would take it if it meant they could get to safety.

"Go, go, go," said Rob, waving his hand in a forwards

direction.

They began crossing the street, the dead's voices even louder now the trio were out in the open. There was a chorus of groans and growls, and when they neared the other side, a loud crack rang out, sending chills down Rob's spine. *Poor souls.*

"Rob!" whispered Jack. "Rob!"

Rob spun around and held his finger up to his lips, signalling for Jack to join him upfront. They all knelt in front of another hedge, clear of the street they had crossed.

"Shouldn't we help them?" asked Jack.

"Help who? We don't even know if anyone is in there. They might have already left through the front just like we did." Rob looked left and right over and over, studying the area. "And how can we help? We're running for our lives, remember?"

"I know, I just thought…"

"We've gotta keep moving, Jack. Right now, it's only about us." Rob put his hand on Jack's arm and nudged him forwards once again. "Come on, let's go." *God, my brother has a heart of gold. Between him and Anna, I've got my work cut out for me.*

* * *

They continued in the same way for another three blocks of houses. Anna looked around, taking in the empty streets, and wondered how many people were still in their own homes, watching them behind curtains. *We must look completely crazy even attempting to be out here.* The only noises now were those of their own feet as they scurried along the footpaths.

83

Anna decided to put Logan down for a little while to walk and run with them, but if shit hit the fan, she would pick him up again. They continued onwards down this block with stealth, whilst Anna held on to the little boy's hand like a vice. *His hand is so tiny in mine, and cold too.* Jasper's hands were pretty beefy, but this little boy was on the dainty side, which only endeared him further to Anna.

Rob was in front, then Jack, followed by Anna and Logan. Anna threw glances over her shoulder every ten seconds just to make sure there weren't any dead behind. The next house they passed had a high hedge, overgrown to where the entrance was covered over a little. The leafy smells of the enormous hedges filled Anna's nose when they drew near.

Rob walked past it first, but as Jack followed, a zombie leapt out from between the branches, heading straight for him. He was looking the other way across the street. It reached out for Jack's head, and Anna saw the movement. She released Logan's tiny hand and lunged at the creature.

Its fingertips brushed Jack's hair, but Anna reached it just in time. She threw herself at it, pushing it back into the garden from where it had emerged.

"Aargh!"

They landed on the ground with Anna on top and no weapon to hand once again. *Fuck! Why do I keep doing this?* She had the hammer in her belt loop, but that would've meant releasing the beast beneath her long enough to get it out. Instead, she held on for dear life.

Anna pushed hard at the writhing monster, whose hands were clawing at her arms, trying to reach her flesh. She looked down at its face long enough to see that it had once been an elderly man with not many teeth left in his mouth. Anna was sure that he wouldn't have had this strength before he was infected. *How on earth does a nice old man turn into a flesh-eating monster? What fucked up world are we in now?*

"Move your face away," said Rob from out of nowhere.

Anna did as she was told, then an almighty whack hit the beast. Anna felt everything stop in that instant. The fury. The hunger. And the fear from herself. She looked back at the monsters face; the writhing had stopped and now the face looked almost serene. She breathed a heavy sigh and dismounted the creature. Rob wiped his hatchet on the dead's clothes, then held his hand towards Anna. She took it and looked up into his smiling face, allowing him to pull her up off the ground. His hand was strong and calloused, but so warm. *Just the way I like them.*

Once she was standing again, she noticed Rob hadn't yet released her. Looking into his eyes, she could see that he wanted to say something to her but couldn't quite get the words out. Anna smiled, letting him know he didn't have to say anything at all. She grasped his warm hand between the two of hers, squeezing them gently before walking back over to where Jack and Logan stood.

"Bloody hell! Thanks, Anna, that nearly had me then," said Jack.

"Hey, I owed you one—big time."

"Nah."

Rob joined them. "Come on, then, let's get moving again before we're seen out here."

Anna took Logan's hand again, and they all continued to the end of the next block, then the one after that until they came to a more expansive open space. There was a large grassed area next to a pub and an underpass. Rob peered around the corner.

"There's a load of 'em near the pub doors at the other side," said Rob.

He rubbed his stubble and looked at the ground. Anna gave Logan's hand to Jack and edged nearer the corner for a look herself. There were six of the dead hanging around near the other side of the pub, right where they would need to walk by.

"Hmm, I see what you mean. And who's to say there aren't more around that corner too," Anna said.

"Exactly," replied Rob.

"What about crossing the grassed area towards those fences over there? It would mean heading back into the estate and rat runs, but it would keep us away from that group, and hopefully they won't be able to see us. I'm certain we could get around the back of that fenced area and come out into one of the streets, which would then lead us back onto the main road again," explained Anna.

Rob's eyes were looking intense again, but he nodded at her that they should try it. "Ok."

Jack put Logan on his back this time, handing over his and Anna's backpacks. Rob took one of the bags off Anna and gave her cricket bat back. "I think you should carry this now."

"Yeah, maybe I should," she replied.

"Ok, everybody ready? Let's do this." Rob lead the group out into the open, and they all darted across the small field, praying they would not be seen.

That was when Logan let out a small child's scream that sent a jolt of terror through them all.

Chapter 10

"**S**HIT! RUN!" shouted Rob.

Two, then three, then four of the dead careened around the corner of the pub, running straight at them. Rob positioned himself between his brother and the monsters heading towards them. Anna's head twisted wildly taking in the position of the advancing zombies and Rob. *He's put himself in the way on purpose.* They all stretched out their legs, sprinting towards the fenced area.

"Over there, we can climb over that gate," Anna shouted as they ran.

They puffed and grunted, which was more to do with the chasers than the actual running. The thought of being eaten alive wasn't the nicest of ways to go, which in turn did seem to get your heart pumping more than usual.

Anna hit the six-foot fence first and knelt on one knee, clasping both of her hands together for Jack. *God, I hope there's nothing inside there.* The gate was the more accessible part to climb over, having a foothold part way up. Jack hurriedly lowered Logan and stepped into Anna's hands, allowing her to push him up, propelling him over the fence. Rob hit the fence in the next few beats but stood sentry, keeping their pursuers in his field of vision whilst he checked out the other directions.

Jack dropped to the other side as Anna lifted Logan high, helping him climb the top part. Jack reached up and lowered him down the other side again. Rob spun around and dropped to one knee, just the way Anna had for Jack. *He's always going to be the last one over, that seems to be who he is.*

Anna stepped into Rob's hands and pushed herself up to the foothold, then over the fence. Then she looked towards the dead and noticed others had joined them. They were close, too damn close, and she wasn't sure Rob was going to make it. *I've got to do something.*

Anna threw herself onto the ground on the other side then sprinted the length of the fence, nearer to the running dead people. She started shouting and waving her arms through the gaps, trying to get the monsters' attention before they reached Rob's location.

"Come on you pieces of shit, live bait right here."

* * *

Rob had got himself halfway up the gate when one of the dead reached him, latching onto his foot and pulling him down again. *Fuck!* The others had noticed Anna and ran at her instead. Rob landed on the ground with a heavy thud, but more importantly, with a crazed, bloodthirsty thing on top of him.

He thrust his forearm up under its chin and pushed the thing off, rolling over on top of it, then pulled out his hatchet with one hand whilst his other held the zombie down on the ground. Rob struck it clean in the head and jumped back up to attack the gate once more. His eyes darted around; a further two beasts were charging at him. His hands shook a little, but he would use the energy to get his arse over that fence.

Rob got himself up high enough this time before they reached the gate. He dropped down to the other side to join Jack and Logan before Anna ran up to them too. Rob's keen eyes assessed the fenced-in area they were now in. *Danger could still be around the corner*, but before Rob could know anything about it, Jack threw himself at his brother in an almighty hug.

"Woah! I'm alright, Jack. Don't worry, those things aren't taking me out, not a chance."

Anna and Rob shared a knowing look; they were beginning to form a pretty good team, and he liked how it felt.

"What took you so long?" Anna teased.

"Ha, I thought you liked a bit of drama. I decided to put on a show for ya," said Rob.

"Yeah, right, it looked more like you fell off the fence."

"Whatever."

They all shared a small, breathless chuckle. Rob looked around the courtyard they were stood in, then back at the ghouls on the other side. There was no way they were getting through that; it was a solid metal fence. They were safe for now, but he still didn't like that they could be seen by them, growling and drawing more to their location. *Why do they have to make such an awful noise?*

"We had better move again and see what's on the other side of this building," said Rob.

Jack and Anna nodded whilst Anna retook Logan's hand.

"How are you doing, little guy?" Anna asked the boy, who just looked up with more tears in his eyes. "Oh, honey. Come here." Anna handed Jack her bat and picked Logan up, wrapping his legs around her body with his face buried in her chest. Rob looked on, knowing full well that Logan had found a worthy woman to care for him. She was motherly in all the right ways, but fierce too. Her strength reminded him dearly of his own mum in the early then later years.

* * *

They walked around the side of the building, Anna cuddling Logan close. This was the next best thing for her to having her own two children to cuddle. The ache she had in her chest only intensified with time, even though they were making progress. She nestled her head against the top of Logan's, breathing in his shampoo, and prayed to God she would see her kids again. Getting this little boy to safety was also a must.

They approached the next corner, and Anna raised her head. She needed to be ready in case anything was inside here. Rob did the reccy around the corner and signalled the all-clear. *He makes me feel so much safer.* They were on the other side of the large building now and only had the fence to climb back out onto the unsafe streets again.

Anna thought about the direction they were now headed whilst breathing in the still fresh morning air. If they cut through a few more streets, they would come out at the old track, which would lead them straight to Steve's back fence. The track was the old railway line that ran from Hull to

Hornsea. It was now called the Trans Pennine Line, but locals would always know it as the track. Old memories surfaced of walking the length of it with her parents one hot summer's day, much like this one so far. Even the smells in the air seemed the same. *Maybe that's why I'm remembering them.*

"Where is it that you guys are heading to? Because Steve's house is roughly in that direction. If we can hit the track, then it'll lead us straight there," said Anna.

"My mate's house isn't far past the track," replied Rob.

"Oh," Anna was taken aback; she hadn't realised Rob had an actual destination in mind. "You know, you guys are more than welcome to join us. First at Steve's, then at his parents. It's a big house with extra annexes, and anyone who helped me the way you guys have would have a place there too."

"Wow, that's incredibly kind of you, Anna." Rob looked down at his feet for a second. "But I think we're better off going to my mates like we had planned. Thank you, though."

Anna swallowed. "No problem. The offer's still open if you change your mind, anyway."

Anna stepped away to stare off into the distance, leaving Rob looking at her back.

"Right, if the coast is clear, we need to get over this fence again, don't we?" Anna asked, without turning back towards both Jack and Rob.

"Yep, that's the plan," replied Rob.

They all scanned the area beyond the fence. There were double gates on this side, so they chose that point to climb over.

"I'll go over first," said Rob.

Jack bent his knee, adopting the leg-up position, and Rob propelled himself over the gate with ease. Jack nodded at

Anna, who placed Logan down before helping Jack over too. Next, Logan was lifted over with Rob on lookout before Anna managed to climb over herself. She grunted and moaned a little, but thanks to her long legs, she managed. *So much bloody climbing!*

They all faced the next street they had to enter. Anna was starting to feel exhausted, not really from the physical exertions but more so from the mental strain this was having on her.

"That way, I guess." Anna pointed between some houses and hoped beyond measure that the street beyond would be empty. Still, she retrieved her bat, and Jack piggybacked Logan. She looked at the three males in front of her and realised she had begun to care for them. They had already gone through so much together; a bond was forming, for sure. *How can I simply walk away from Rob and Jack after all we've been through?*

They began moving along a line of fences and hedges, making their way over to the next corner. There was a smaller four-foot fence to climb over, so Rob signalled for everyone to wait behind it whilst he checked it out. Anna eyed the space they had just crossed, checking for any movement.

Rob beckoned them all over the fence and to the corner he stood at.

"It looks clear as far as I can see, so let's move," said Rob.

They moved as one, silently and efficiently to the next enclosed footpath between two rows of houses. At another four-foot fence, Rob repeated the last set of actions. They made their way through another two streets in much the same way, getting ever closer to the track and Anna's temporary haven. *Getting closer all the time, but it still feels like a million miles away from my children. Just gotta stay alert, and make sure we all get there safe.*

Two of the dead walked by a little farther down the street, grunting, shuffling, and chomping their jaws, so the team paused where they were. Anna looked towards the opening and the road beyond. They all looked the same in these areas; council built housing where many had purchased their own. There was the occasional gem amongst the rougher houses, too, where the owners put a loving stamp on it.

For most people who live around these parts, the only real thing they possess is their home, even when it's rented. Could this be the end of society as we know it, or would the Armed Forces be able to pull civilisation back? *If they can, surely they should be getting a bloody move on by now.*

It wasn't long before the dead they were hiding from heard something and went hurtling off. They crossed the street together and came to a much larger fence this time. It was one without footholds, so it would be more difficult to mount for the last one over.

Anna stepped forward to go over first. Rob knelt for her, and she mounted the fence well. She dropped down, then Rob lifted Logan up for Anna to take hold of. She struggled a little more than Jack had, not having Jack's few extra inches of height. Then Jack passed the cricket bat through the gaps in the metal fencing.

Rob began to turn away from Anna to give Jack his leg up when he suddenly spun back to look over Anna's shoulder. Anna understood Rob's face in a flash as he lunged at the fence, grabbing the bars and shouting her name. She didn't hear it, though, she could only hear the growl behind her getting closer. *I'm on my own.*

Chapter 11

Rob's eyes widened, taking in the view behind Anna. He wanted to run to her and Logan, to save them both. They were on the other side of the bars, but whatever he did, it would be too late. *Or would it?* Grabbing the bars, he shouted her name, then looked up at the fence.

Anna began to turn towards her threat.

"Rob!" said Jack.

Rob spun around to view their side of the fence; two hungry beasts were heading their way. *SHIT!* He did a quick double take, but it was no use. He wanted to help Anna and Logan, but there was no way he could leave Jack to these two things. They bared their teeth and reached out their arms, picking up speed.

Rob released the bars and spun to face the dead, taking his first step forwards. He pulled the hatchet from his holster with his right hand and simultaneously pushed Jack towards the fence with his left, giving him the room he needed to work.

A snarl spread across Rob's face, releasing an angry growl of his own as he strode forwards. He needed to dispatch these things quickly so he could get over to Anna and Logan. *No fucking way am I gonna watch a child die today.*

The first dead thing had almost reached him when he placed his left foot forward and swung his right arm back and low. He released a powerful swipe upwards through the first attacker's face, which sent it flying backwards and hitting the wall on its way down. Blood flung off of the hatchet as it swung its arc away from the zombie. Rob capitalised on his hatchet and arm's position and threw a deadly backhand into the skull of the second beast. *Take that, you fucker.*

The hatchet embedded firmly into its skull and stopped it in its tracks. Rob yanked the hatchet out of its head as the first creature was rising from the ground. Rob knew he hadn't killed it the first time because he'd only hit its jaw, not wanting the hatchet to get stuck with the second beast approaching. He could now finish it off with a forceful whack to the forehead.

He felt like a madman as he pulled his hatchet free and rotated to see Anna and Logan, praying to God he could get over the fence in time. *Just hold on, guys.*

* * *

The raspy dead thing was heading their way with its teeth and grasping hands ready for her and Logan. She began to turn her head, and her eyes crossed Logan's small frame backing up into the corner of the fence and the wall. She caught the look of terror in his eyes and felt a fire beginning within her.

He's done nothing to deserve any of this—and neither have I, come to think of it. My children need me, and now Logan does too. She directed her gaze at the creature in front of her before grasping her cricket bat like a baseball player, moving forwards and meeting it partway down the alley.

She had timed it perfectly, planting her left foot in front of her and readying herself for the swing. The cricket bat swiped through the air, hitting the beast's head with a crack and a grunt from Anna. The skull did not fully break, though, it simply bounced off the nearest wall, so Anna pulled back the bat for another swing. She held her breath, then unleashed another blow at its head. She let out a repressed scream, but not too loud. The second hit made it topple to the ground.

Anna didn't know if it was dead or not, so she stood straddling it with the bat held high over her head. She sucked in a lungful of air and pushed it out with all of her might, pummelling its head. Blow, after blow, Anna's crazed eyes looked on as she pounded it into oblivion. *Fucking die.*

The brain was like mush, spreading out onto the ground around the head. Anna realised she was now hitting the tarmac and no longer the dead thing's skull, so she pulled back, stepping over the body lying beneath her. The smell of blood reached her nose, as had a putrid one when she straddled it.

Anna panted, feeling warm tears over her cheeks. *Oh my God, stop fucking crying you useless bitch.* But she couldn't tear her eyes from it laying there motionless on the ground. It used to be a man, wearing jeans and a T-shirt with Iron Maiden on the front. *He used to be someone's son.*

She finally stepped away and lifted her head, looking out of the alleyway, making sure nothing else was going to follow. She was back from her zone out and ready to take on more if she needed to. *I can do this.*

Anna's hands were shaking, so she gripped the cricket bat firmer. She used one hand to touch her locket momentarily;

it's almost becoming a habit now, she thought. Her whole body was trembling too. *I imagine this is typical for this kind of trauma*, she told herself. But she knew she had done what she needed to. She lifted her head, willing the shaking to subside.

* * *

Rob spun away from his own fallen creatures and ran to the fence, taking in the scene before him. His arms had already begun reaching upwards to scale the fence when he realised Anna and Logan were still standing and the beast was not. He leant to look around Anna and let out a soft chuckle at the mess covering the ground in front of her.

"Holy shit," said Rob.

"Yeah, she was immense," replied Jack, who had witnessed everything. "I did start to climb over to help them, but I realised she didn't need it."

"Let's get you over now, then."

Rob gave Jack a leg up to climb the fence and drop onto the other side to join Anna and Logan. Rob's muscles made following look easy. Jack went straight to Logan who was still cowering in the corner of the fence and the wall, and squatted in front of him.

"Hey, Logan, you're ok, mate. Look, Anna's a total badass," said Jack, pointing to her. "She smashed that thing into smithereens."

Logan threw himself at Jack and held on for dear life. Rob tore his eyes away from how good his little brother was with kids. He allowed a slight grin before approaching Anna who stood stock still further down the pathway between the houses still. He reached out his hand and touched her arm. Anna spun her head around to face him.

"Hey, you ok?" asked Rob.

Anna never spoke; instead, she let out a long breath with her eyes closed. Rob closed the distance between them and lowered his head to look at her eyes better. He smiled into her face, wanting to make her smile too.

"Anna, you did it. You pounded the bastard. Look, he doesn't even have much of a head anymore." Rob let out a small laugh. "There's no way I'm getting into any more arguments with you, that's for sure."

Anna's smile flittered across her face whilst she wiped her eyes, removing any traces of tears. With another huge breath out, she stepped closer to Rob, resting her head on his shoulder. He breathed in the smell of her hair and let her have just a moment of silence before he knew they had to get moving again. His hand stroked her back, then patted it.

"Come on," he said.

Anna lifted her head and gave a firm nod. Rob beckoned Jack and Logan over, and they all geared up to prepare for the next street. Jack put Logan on his back, and on Rob's ok, they all ran across the next road.

The rat runs had ended, but they were still in the middle of the housing estates—still too many people. They crossed another main road that ringed the rat runs known as Biggin Avenue and headed towards the street that would lead them onto the track.

* * *

They travelled in silence for a few hundred metres before a scream rang out, and they all twisted in the direction it had come from. Jack was at the group's rear and could see a girl being pinned down back across the road, not far from them. The creature was on top and nearing her face, snapping its jaws at her and trying to reach her in any way it could. The girl pushed at it with both of her hands. *I can help her.*

Jack bolted across the road to help the girl.

"Jack, no!" Rob warned in a whisper shout.

Jack didn't look back; he just continued forwards until he reached them, swinging his right boot at the head of the creature. He struck it well, just under its chin, launching it off the girl. It flew to the side, and the girl scrabbled away. Jack followed the beast and connected his foot with its head again. It landed on its back this time, so Jack wasted no time slamming his Timberland down onto its face three times before it stopped moving.

Jack stepped away from it, panting heavily but ready to strike again. He hovered his hand over the hatchet at his waist, but had no need to draw. He looked down at the mess he had created and nodded to himself. *I am EPIC! Where's the next female I can save?*

The girl scurried off. Jack twisted his head and noticed her running around a corner, away from him. He was about to follow when he felt a hand on his arm.

"Do. Not. Do. That. Again," Rob said through gritted teeth.

Jack grinned from ear to ear, not caring that Rob was pissed. "Shut up, Rob. Did you not see what I did? I was awesome."

Rob put his hand to his head and looked to the floor, slowly shaking it from side to side. "Just… move back over the road, for God's sake."

Rob and Jack rejoined Anna and Logan, who were crouching near some bushes.

"Did you see that, Anna?" Jack asked, hyped-up, bouncing from foot to foot.

"Uh-huh, I certainly did." Anna flashed Jack a small smile and a wink when Rob wasn't looking. *I knew she'd be impressed,* thought Jack.

"We'd better get away from here before the girl's screams draw more of those things," said Rob, giving his brother the side-eye.

Jack raised his eyebrows at Anna, and they all moved onwards again.

* * *

The four of them dodged and weaved their way through the next street. Bodies littered the road and grassed verges. It appeared whatever had gone down was now over for the time being. *Maybe the dead things have moved on to another area,* Anna hoped.

They were about to emerge onto the next street from Steve's when Rob hushed them all and shoved them back behind some bushes. A herd of the beasts ran by, but Anna couldn't see who they were chasing.

Then the vehicle's engine revved far too loud. *Bloody hell, those things have got fantastic hearing.* Anna frowned, realising this was another point in favour of the dead. Blowing out a lungful of air, Anna continued to peek through the bushes until Rob gave the all-clear.

They hurried across the road and entered the track. The first part wasn't covered over well, leaving them all too exposed. Anna's gaze shifted left and right every second they were out in the open.

She looked over at Jack, who was clinging on to Logan's hand. The little guy had managed to keep up with them as they jogged down the pathway and had been so quiet. The boy had adapted to his new world far too quickly, in Anna's opinion. She raised her eyes heavenwards. *Please, God, don't let things stay like this.*

Anna checked her watch and realised it was still only morning. They neared Steve's house, and her heart rate picked up with desperation clawing its way up her spine. *Nearly there, nearly there, nearly there.* Her mind chanted it over and over. *Please, let us get there.*

Chapter 12

They continued down the track, nearing Anna's ex-partner's house. It was a long stretch of footpath in a straight line, allowing them a good view of what might be in front. Bushes and trees lined it either side, in full bloom. Much of the foliage was giving off a floral scent that Anna couldn't place. Beyond were garden fences and people's houses; Anna wondered how many people were still in their homes.

They were nearing Steve's fence—it was another two hundred metres away—when Rob spotted a zombie on the path. He directed them all behind a large bush and some trees, pointing it out to them. Anna peered through the branches, feeling one brush against her hair. She looked up towards the sky and could feel the sun on her face. Had it been an average day, she might have been sat in her garden, reading a book and letting the sun caress her skin. *Not today, though. Will I ever again?*

"Shit, it's almost where we need to be," said Anna.

"Really? What are the chances?" answered Rob, shaking his head.

"Well, there's a path coming from the left side there, leading onto this track from another area of houses. There could be more of them down that path that we can't see until we're on top of it."

"Bugger," said Rob.

"Yeah, I agree."

"Let's wait it out a bit and see if they wander off," said Rob.

"Ok," Anna agreed. It's not like they had anything better to do.

They shuffled Jack and Logan into the back of the bushes whilst Anna and Rob remained nearer the front, hunched over and ready to act if needed. Their heads were very close now, and Anna could feel Rob's breath on the side of her neck. *Was he looking at her?*

Anna left it a few more seconds before turning to face him. He *had* been staring at her and looked away quickly, so Anna faced back towards the dead with a smile playing against the sides of her mouth. She could feel butterflies in her tummy with Rob being so close. *Oh my God, I'm like a schoolgirl. Get a grip, Anna,* she told herself.

Anna knew they would be parting ways soon, anyway. She breathed out a slow breath, trying to push away the urge to turn and look at his face. Just once, she wanted to see those eyes again before shit could hit the fan and she lost her chance. She chewed on her lip whilst thinking things over.

She eventually decided she needed to say something to Rob. "In case all of this goes south quickly, I'd just like to say that it's been a pleasure knowing you and Jack. You are both so… amazing, I can't even find the right words." Anna stifled the tears that threatened to start. "What I'm trying to say is… Thank you, both of you. You saved me many times over, something I can never repay." Anna looked at the floor, feeling more emotional than she would have thought. *These life and death situations really do get to you.*

Anna heard Rob run the palm of his hand over his stubble and cursed herself for saying anything. But suddenly, he cupped Anna's chin, turning her face towards his. She looked straight into those vibrant green eyes and melted. His hand was so gentle, but she wanted more.

"No need to say thanks; you saved Jack, too, remember. You're an amazing woman, Anna, and I know you will get your kids to safety; I have no doubt about that." He looked away for a moment, and Anna felt desperate for his eyes to find hers again. He said, "Never doubt yourself. *You...* can do anything, anything at all." *The exact opposite of what Steve had said.*

Rob's eyes searched her face, and she noticed he was looking at her mouth. She looked at his mouth, too, feeling the pull there. Anna didn't think at all; she leant in, pressing her lips against his and closing her eyes, just for a moment. She could forget where they were and what was going on around them. Zone out and ignore the mumbling zombies farther down the footpath.

His hand found the back of her head and pulled her closer, kissing her deeper before caressing her cheek. Anna sighed into him, breathing heavily and taking her time. Then her hand grasped onto his jacket and held on for dear life. *I wanted this so much, now I don't want to let go.*

"Er, hello! Dead people who want to eat us out there," Jack interrupted, sounding very jovial.

Rob pulled back from the kiss and cleared his throat before throwing his brother daggers. Anna pressed her lips together, trying not to laugh or smile too hard, and looked back over to

104

where a second creature had joined its friend.

"Oh, shit! There's a second one now. They must be milling around down the alleyway," said Anna, hoping her voice wasn't wavering after that intense moment she and Rob had just shared.

"Yeah—" Rob sounded gruff and cleared his throat before he could say more "—they must be."

Anna looked back to Rob and couldn't help the huge smile that spread across her face. Rob's mouth mirrored Anna's, and then just like that, the moment had passed, and they had to get back to business.

* * *

Rob's heart was going to pound right out of his chest. *What a kiss! I never expected that, but I'm over the moon she did it. I'm not sure I'd have had the guts to do it.* It was all he could think about until Anna pulled his attention back to the job at hand. Two dead could turn into three, or four, or even more. At what point should they decide to just dispatch them before more came to join the party? *Do we always continue to run, or do we start being the aggressors for a change?*

"I reckon we could take the two of 'em between us," suggested Rob, looking for approval from Anna. "I say we leave these two in the bushes here, well hidden, and go get them. As long as we leave enough of a gap between us and the side path, then even if more filter out of it, we still have the option to run."

Anna waved her arms around a little. "Er... really? Are you mad?"

Rob sent a firm nod her way. "We'll be ok. I've seen what you can do with that thing." He pointed to Anna's cricket bat.

"Ok, I guess. I can't think of any better ideas." She scratched her head. "I don't relish the thought of attacking them, but… yeah, let's do it."

"It'll be ok, I promise. You'll be amazing, I'm sure of it," said Rob.

Anna smiled at him, and he loved it. "I can certainly try, anyway. You might just have to rescue me again, though, if it does goes wrong," she said.

"It's not gonna go wrong." Rob looked towards his brother. "Jack, you ok with this?"

"I reckon so. Just make sure you come back for us," said Jack, tucking himself and Logan farther back into the bushes.

"Keep a close watch out, though, because if things go tits up, we're gonna need to leg it. Watch the other direction, too, and give us a whistle if you see anything," said Rob.

"Ok, no problemo, big brother." Jack saluted them.

Rob inched farther out toward the path, looking in the opposite direction to the dead. The track they had recently run down was still empty. He needed this to go right because Anna needed it for so many reasons.

He looked at his brother and couldn't believe how grown up he seemed now, after just a short while out in this crazy world. Rob twisted his head the other way; there were still only the two creatures wandering around. *Time for action.*

"Right, you ready?" he said, raising his eyebrows at Anna.

"Ready as I'll ever be," she replied, still chewing on her lower lip.

She gripped the bat, causing her knuckles to whiten. He hadn't ever been an affectionate guy, but seeing Anna's nerves made him want to be. He reached out his hand to cover hers, flashing her a winning smile and a wink.

He threw another quick look in both directions and stepped out into the open. Anna followed, and they walked towards the dead, knowing full well what they were about to do.

* * *

Oh, shitting hell, what I have just agreed to? Anna thought, matching Rob's pace, stride for stride. *You've done it before; you can do it again,* she told herself. *Yeah, when I absolutely had to... Oh bugger, I'm arguing with myself now. Just shut up and focus!*

Anna strived to bring her attention back around and looked straight at the things they were about to attack. She couldn't help reaching for the locket she still had hanging around her neck, a reminder of her reasons for everything she had done so far and anything else that would arise.

The dead hadn't noticed them yet, but it would only be a matter of seconds before they did. She looked down at her bat, feeling its weight, and adjusted her grip, then looked across at Rob, who looked more than ready to kill these beasts. He held his hatchet in his right hand, which was hanging loosely by his side. His eyes were on his targets, unblinking. *Ok, Anna, no more blinking!*

"They've seen us," said Rob.

"K,"

There's no point wasting energy on useless words; it's only action that counts now. Please help me do this, God! If there is a God, anyway. Anna couldn't stop the thoughts in her head. Round and round they went as the beasts began running at them.

Shaking her mind clear, Rob said, "You step to the right, and I'll step to the left, then we'll have one each."

Anna followed his instructions. The beasts neared, so she gripped the bat in both of her hands, raising it level with her head. Hers was a woman when she was alive, wearing a smart skirt and blouse, but no shoes. *She must have lost them. Fuck it, FOCUS!* Anna screamed at herself inside of her mind.

Off to her left side, she caught sight of Rob dashing forwards, almost launching himself at his beast. Anna brought her attention back to hers and backed off a pace, allowing herself that one more moment before she had to strike.

Clunk! The bat's sound on the dead things head was almost comical, and Anna had to repress the urge to giggle. Maybe it was slight hysteria, but she knew she had to do this. For herself, for her kids, and for Logan. They all needed her strength, so she had to find it somewhere.

It stumbled to Anna's left and hadn't quite righted its footing when Anna kicked at its left knee, sending it crashing to the ground like a sack of potatoes. It tried to stand again when Anna swung the bat at its face, smashing the nose with a crunch and a squelch. It toppled backwards, and its head hit the ground. Anna wasted no time in running over and using the end of the bat to pound through its skull into the brain. More squelching over and over.

Anna started to step away, feeling somewhat satisfied with herself, when a loud growl shocked her into turning around. Another dead person was immediately on her. She managed to bring the bat up in front of herself with both hands, pushing it back a little. Anna was shocked at the sheer strength of the dead once again as its weight pushed her back.

Think Anna! Their only focus is trying to bite flesh, but we can think outside of the box. Anna released her hands from the bat and, at the same time, flung herself to the right. The creature went flying forwards and stumbled to the ground, still clinging to Anna's bat.

She ran at it and slammed her boot down onto its head again and again until it remained still. The feeling of smashing a person's head in would surely never leave her; it was disgusting. Anna spun round to see Rob fighting off two of the dead at the same time. *I guess there* were *more down the alleyway.*

Anna rolled the dead creature off her bat, trying not to look at its mangled head, and ran to join Rob. He had managed to push one away whilst he embedded his hatchet into another. The thrown beast was just about to grab Rob from behind when Anna whacked it around the head, sending it sideways.

She wasted no time whacking it again, making the beast crumple to the ground, where she finished it off with a couple more hearty hits. The thuds reverberated through her whole body, and she began to feel the weight of the wood in her hands.

Sweat was pouring off her; swinging a bat was hard work. With the sun high in the sky, it was sure to be a hot day. She scanned the track and realised they had finished off those they needed to. Anna looked to the floor and breathed an exaggerated breath outwards. Thankfully, no more were coming at them.

Rob looked over to Anna with a grin and said, "Yep, pretty badass."

Anna found herself laughing. "You're not too bad yourself."

Chapter 13

Rob waved Jack and Logan over, and they all stalked past the path that fed onto the track. All in all, they had offed seven of the dead, the hidden path having concealed them. They dodged the mess covering the ground on the way to Steve's back fence. One of the dead things had half of its guts hanging out, so Anna tried not to breathe through her nose.

They all huddled in the bushes that backed onto Steve's garden.

"Well, this is me," Anna said with a mixture of feelings. How could she explain that she didn't want them to leave right now, that it felt wrong on many levels? She had developed a firm bond with them both and hated having to say goodbye. She looked at Jack, then dragged him into a hug. "Thank you, Jack. I will never forget you." She kissed him on the cheek, then released him. He chose to look at his shoes and not respond. Anna took it as a sign that he was feeling a little emotional.

"If you guys change your mind at all, you should head over to Preston. It's the largest property on the main street with a massive brown fence and gate that rings the grounds. It's set back amongst loads of trees, too, so it's kind of hidden at the same time." Anna searched Rob's face for any indication he might decide to join them.

"Thanks, Anna. Good luck to you and your family," replied Rob.

Rob had also decided this was an excellent time to look at *his* shoes. Anna had hoped for a bit more from him in this instance, but she knew there was no topping their earlier moment. They were parting ways, never to meet again, so what was the point, anyway? Anna had decided shortly after separating from Steve that she didn't need or want another man in her life for a long time. *I can't believe I got so attached so quickly... What's wrong with me?*

Anna paused before speaking again in a quiet manner. "Ok, then. Come on, Logan, this is where we go over the fence."

Anna had a quick peek over, checking the garden was clear. The curtains were drawn over the large patio doors, and she prayed they were all safe inside. Rob walked over and stood directly in front of Anna, with their faces only inches away. Anna's mouth dropped open a little, and she held her breath, hoping he was going to say something to her. Instead, he squatted down, offering a leg up. *Hmm...*

Anna studied him whilst he avoided her face once again. She released the breath she had been holding and decided to just get on with it, stepping into his hands. She mounted the fence from there and landed on the grass in the garden. After a quick look left and right, assessing the neighbouring houses and gardens, she concluded that it was safe for Logan to join her.

"Ok, ready for Logan," said Anna.

Logan was lifted over, and Anna placed him down on the grass next to herself. She watched him whilst he looked around. *What are you thinking, little man?* Anna reached out and stroked his hair, hoping he would be ok with them.

"Bye, Anna. Good luck," whispered Jack through the fence.

Anna looked up and could see his hand there waving at them. She said, "Bye, Jack, take care of your brother for me."

"I will," he replied.

"Bye, Rob, maybe see you around," said Anna, hoping so much that would be true somehow.

"Yeah. Bye, Anna. Take care," replied Rob in a muted and dreary voice.

Anna pressed her hand against her side of the fence and blew out a breath of air. She could hear them running down the path and missed them already. She then faced Steve's house and grasped Logan's hand tenderly. She collected her bat from the ground, and they marched to the patio doors, where she tapped lightly on the glass.

She stepped back, looking up in case Steve was looking out of the upstairs window. The curtain moved the tiniest fraction. *Oh my God, they're still here.* She looked around the garden and fence to the side and could see no damage of any kind, so all must be ok inside. *Please be ok.*

The curtain was flung back, and there stood her two beautiful children, staring up like she had popped round for a visit and they didn't know why. Anna raised her face to the sky and closed her eyes tight against the tears that were brewing there. Steve slid the door open steadily, trying not to make a noise. Anna and Logan stepped inside, closing the door behind them.

* * *

Rob and Jack exited the track just a couple of hundred metres farther on and crouched down near some bushes. Rob wanted to assess the big open street they had to travel down. It was a wide street that usually saw plenty of traffic, and it had trees lining most of it, with a large park to the right. His friend's house wasn't too much farther—just a few streets away, in fact.

Rob was looking around but could feel his brow scrunched up. He had been clenching his teeth together, too, ever since leaving Anna and Logan.

"What's up with you? Your face looks like you're chewing a wasp," said Jack, staring into his brother's eyes.

"Just leave it, Jack," replied Rob.

Jack raised his eyebrows and looked away. The truth was that Rob had felt like crap ever since they had got Anna to her ex's house. He hated seeing her jump over *his* fence, and he absolutely hated walking away from them both.

He looked off into the distance to avoid Jack's gaze and thought about their kiss. He hadn't had that kind of affinity to another human being for a long time, if ever. It was crazy, because he didn't really know her properly; just those last few hours together seemed enough, though. *Which is why I had to walk away. Never get too close, Rob!*

Rob had witnessed his mum display poor judgement time and time again when it came down to the opposite sex. She ultimately lost herself for many years, which meant he and Jack had lost her too. She did find her way back, but Rob could never forget how it felt to witness her so upset.

He vowed to never allow himself to be sucked in by other people, even if it meant he was often alone. Rob chose a select few close friends, and that was it. And hardly ever a woman; they were just way too much hassle. But Anna, she had crept inside just a tiny bit. *I have to stick to the plan... Do not get attached.*

"Where is it that we're going again?" asked Jack.

"To my mate's house. You remember Andy, don't you?" replied Rob.

"No, not really. And why are we going?" queried Jack, like he was trying to aggravate his brother.

Rob took a deep breath so he didn't snap and said, "Well, little brother, I reckon he's in the know about what's going down right now. Not to mention the fact that he'll probably have a small arsenal in his little semi-detached. Safest to place to be, in my opinion."

"Uh-huh, and does my opinion count at all?" Jack looked squarely at his older brother now, displaying maturity that Rob never knew existed.

"Nope," replied Rob, turning to continue scouring the streets around them.

Jack sucked on his teeth—something Rob chose to ignore. He could see three of the dead along the street, but they were approximately five hundred metres away. He decided the best course of action was to run to the next set of bushes and assess from there. Not something Rob liked to do, but since he had been winging it all morning, he thought he'd give it a try.

"Come on," he said.

They both bolted to the next set of bushes. Rob looked around again and chose the next safe spot. They both ran over to it and shuffled far into the hedge. These bushes and trees backed onto a tall fence, so Rob took a peek over the top. He could see a clear row of gardens all lined up in front of him.

"I think I've just had a good idea," said Rob.

"It had to happen eventually," Jack said with a straight face.

114

Rob punched him on the arm but really wanted to laugh for the first time in a while. He knew how much of a great kid Jack was, and he couldn't be more proud.

"Let's go, funny man, we're going over this fence." Rob gestured towards the garden, eliciting a confused look from Jack.

"Ok, whatever," Jack replied.

Rob helped Jack over the fence, then pulled himself over to join him.

"Why are we in someone's garden?"

Rob shushed him. "Follow me."

Rob walked over to the next fence in front of them and, after checking the coast was clear, directed Jack over it. Rob joined his brother in the second garden and could see Jack was looking down the long line of gardens himself.

"Ahh, I know what we're doing now." Jack waved his finger at his brother with a big grin on his face. "Let's do this."

They travelled in silence over several more garden fences, moving nearer to Andy's house with every new garden they hit. It was slow going, but it kept them much more hidden than the streets. This way, they always had the chance to duck under cover should one of the dead walk on by.

No one ever looked out of their windows at them. Rob wasn't even sure if there was anyone home in most of the houses. Some had their curtains drawn closed the same way Steve had, but many had them wide open. This meant only one thing to Rob; they hadn't made it.

They stood in the last garden on this particular block, and Rob looked at the washing on the line. It was full of toddler and baby clothes. Tiny white onesies, bibs, and small white t-shirts covered the entirety of the line. Their curtains were open, and Rob could only hope they were somewhere else safe. He looked away from the line and towards the next fence.

They traversed several blocks like this until they could see Andy's house up ahead.

"There it is," said Rob, pointing towards a three-bedroom house at the bottom of a cul-de-sac. "Just stay out of sight a minute while I have a look."

Rob peered over the top of the fence at the bottom of the garden, covered by a monstrous bush. He then narrowed his eyes and descended back towards the ground, where Jack waited for him.

He squatted down with his fingers intertwined and rested his forehead against them. He stared off into space for what seemed like an eternity before muttering, "Shit." He hit his own head before turning to Jack, who looked on concerned.

"What is it? Can I have a look?" Jack said before attempting to rise and see for himself.

"No," said Rob, holding his brother's arm and stopping him from looking over the top of the fence.

"Well, what is it?" asked Jack again.

"It's the stuff of nightmares… that's what it is, Jack."

Chapter 14

"Mummy, I can't breathe," said Jasper.

"Me too," agreed Alex.

"Ok, ok, I'm letting you go now." Anna reluctantly released her two children. She couldn't stop looking at them. Her children were now right in front of her. Her emotions threatened to overwhelm her again. She swiped at her eyes to stop the tears before they flowed fully and took a few deep breaths. She looked towards Logan, who had taken to standing closely behind her, and brought him around in front.

Squatting next to Logan and taking hold of his hand, she said, "Kids, this is Logan. Logan, these are my children, Alex and Jasper."

Alex and Jasper both did a slight wave to him and smiled so sweetly that Anna's heart did a small flip.

"And this is Steve, their daddy," Anna added.

"Er… Hi, Logan," said Steve, scratching his head. He looked down at the little boy, then over to Anna before returning to Logan. "Are you hungry, Logan? I'll bet a strapping boy like you would love a bowl of choco hoops."

"And me, Daddy," said Jasper.

"Alex?" asked Steve.

"Yes, please," she replied.

Steve looked back towards Logan. "Yes, please," said Logan in his quiet voice, but smiling.

"Ok, then, everyone to the table, and remember to be quiet kids. It's very important," reminded Steve.

All three children sat around the kitchen table and waited in silence for their cereal. Steve readied it all, throwing the odd glance at Anna, then back at Logan.

Anna whispered, "I'll tell you soon."

Steve nodded and delivered the midmorning snack to the kids. It was his way of welcoming Logan and keeping them all busy at the same time. Anna removed her backpack, jacket, and hammer from her belt loop. She sighed and rubbed at her eyes before dragging her palms down her face. *I feel so drained. More to come yet, though.*

"Logan, I'm just going to be in the next room while you eat. Alex and Jasper will take good care of you, but if you need anything, just come get me, ok?" said Anna, kneeling next to him at the table.

Logan nodded his approval, so Anna rose and reached out her hand, stroking his head with tenderness before doing the same to Alex and Jasper, with added kisses thrown in too. She breathed in the smell of their hair, then pulled away to join Steve in the next room.

Steve pushed the door towards the frame but never closed it. He faced Anna and looked her up and down. Anna followed his gaze and realised she was looking somewhat dishevelled. Her hands were filthy, so she picked at the grime underneath her varnished nails, then bent down and brushed some of the mud away from her jeans too.

"I'll probably need a wash," suggested Anna.

"Good idea," replied Steve. "How on earth did you get here, Anna? I've been watching out of the windows, and it's been progressively getting worse. I'd started to fear that it was impossible out there." He looked dumbfounded, shaking his head at her.

"Well… I ran," Anna replied, holding out her hands. "I ran a lot, in fact."

She thought back over her whole journey here. *How the hell did I manage it?* Then her face relaxed into a knowing smile, and she said, "And I had help. Two brothers… they saved me. I'm certain I wouldn't be here without them."

"Right… Where are they? And where did Logan come from?" asked Steve.

A wave of sadness swept over Anna's face, thinking of the small boy and his parents. She would look after him now, at least until all of this was over and they could locate some family for him. But if that never happened, Anna would love him as her own.

"I'll tell you all about it soon, Steve, but first I need a wash; I'm filthy," she said.

* * *

Jack peered through a small hole he had found in the fence.

"Holy crap, they got into the house," he whispered, taking in the scene.

Rob pressed his back into the fence and stared at the house in front of him. The curtains open once again and no sign of life inside. He surmised it must be an older couple's house from the décor he could see from his hunched down spot at the foot of the garden.

Pretty flowers lined the sides of the manicured grass, and a miniature greenhouse sat near the house, off to one side. He assumed there would be a couple living here; a place of this size was probably too much for one ageing individual.

"Yeah, I saw that," Rob replied in a quiet voice.

He reminded himself of what Jack was now seeing. The scene flashed up in his mind, shaking him more than anything he had seen so far. The zombies had got inside the house. Every downstairs window was broken, and the door was wide open. *Why was it open? If I have to guess... they tried to make a run for it.*

There was a car just a few feet away from the driveway with two of the doors left wide open. It could have been Andy's car, but Rob didn't know what his friend was driving from one day to the next. He preferred to change his vehicles on a regular basis, unlike Rob, who didn't even own a car.

The dead were milling around inside the house like they were having a party. Curtains were torn and flapping through the holes in the place, and two or three bags littered the front lawn. What deflated him more than the rest of it, though, was the sight of several bodies on the ground. He couldn't see if any were friends or family, but the belief that they could be brought all of their plans crashing down.

Rob was sick to the stomach at the thought of Andy's children being bitten. His wife was the nicest person you could ever meet, too, and as he tried to erase the image of her smiling face from his mind, he knew they must be gone. *How could they have escaped that with three small kids in tow?*

"Do you think they made it out?" asked Jack, looking down at his forlorn brother.

Rob tore his gaze away from the calm house he had been looking at and, meeting his brother's eyes, answered the painful question: "No." Now he was sat still, he could hear the collection of growls on the breeze.

"Oh," Jack replied. "I'm sorry, Rob."

Rob nodded, looking off into the distance once more.

"So, what now?" asked Jack.

Rob shrugged and upturned both of his hands. "I honestly don't know," he said. "Andy was the most prepared person I've ever known, and he couldn't make it."

"What are you saying? That *we* can't make it?"

Rob rubbed his forehead and looked at the ground. *How can I answer that question truthfully without terrifying the lad?*

"I'm not sure," he replied; it was the only answer he could give right now.

"Well, I'm not giving up. You never saw Anna when she was being chased by a hundred of those things. She just ran and ran and ran, not for one second giving up, because if she had, she wouldn't be with her kids right now, would she? She was terrified too; I could see it on her face with every corner we turned. But every time she needed to, she smashed another one of the dead's heads in with that cricket bat. I actually think she might be the bravest person I've ever known." Jack stared Rob in the eyes and jabbed a finger into his chest, saying, "It used to be you."

Jack flared his nostrils, looking agitated, and Rob watched his brother turn away from him. "Wow... that was quite a speech for a gobshite like you." A smile played at the edges of Rob's mouth. *The kid is right, though.*

"I'd rather be a gobshite than an ex-army saddo," replied Jack, giving Rob the side-eye.

Rob chuckled to himself, then said, "Ooh, is that the best you've got?"

"Dude, I haven't even started yet," Jack replied. He still wasn't smiling, but Rob could tell he was finished on his soapbox for now.

"Ok… you're right—unfortunately. We… *I* shouldn't give up. I think we need to take a bit of time to think out our next move." Rob looked back towards the house of the garden they were sat in and nodded to himself. "Let's go in this house 'ere and rest a bit. I could probably think better then."

"*We.* You must mean *we* can think better." Jack glared at Rob.

"Oh bugger, you seem to be right again, you little shitbag," he replied, giving Jack a playful jab on the arm. "Sorry, *dude*."

Rob surveyed the patio doors of the house, looking for a discreet way to enter. They were an old, aluminium frame that didn't have much security about them—the kind that could be lifted out to gain entry. Rob pulled at it, and the outer door did just that. They both entered in silence and with ease, then Rob replaced the useless glass door.

They checked out the downstairs, pulling the curtains together in each room. This house did belong to an older couple. From the table cloth to the wallpaper, it screamed of decades ago. There were also two sets of gardening shoes placed at the back door; one pair was a man's, and the other pair a woman's.

They walked through into the living room to find comfortable seats. Rob looked around the room, taking in the many photos framed on every wall. They had loads of grandchildren, by the looks of it, with some in full family shots and others in single school photos.

Rob was about to take a seat on the floral settee when an audible thud came from above. Both Jack and Rob looked to the ceiling of the small sitting room they now occupied, then back to each other.

"Shit… will this day never end?" complained Rob, looking down at the worn carpet.

Rob grunted before dragging his feet over to the door that separated them from the staircase. He twisted his head to Jack, still occupying the centre of the room and held out his hand, signalling for him to remain where he was. Jack rolled his eyes but never moved.

Rob removed his backpack, pulled out his hatchet, squeezed the door handle, and accessed the hallway with caution. He peered up the stairs for a short beat before ascending; it occurred to him it could be other intruders. *Am I prepared to fight a living person?*

He crept up the stairs, keeping his footing nearer to the walls to avoid any possible creaks that might give him away. There appeared to be four rooms upstairs with just one door closed. He could see a bathroom, an office or study, and what looked like a guest room slash junk room—all with dated décor.

The room with the closed door was at the far end of the landing, so he crept over to it. Rob reached what he assumed was the master bedroom and pressed his ear to the thin plywood, listening out for what or who could be inside.

He remained still for around thirty seconds, listening with eyes narrowed, until hurried footsteps approached from directly behind him, accompanied by a deep-throated growl.

Chapter 15

Anna shared her story with Steve. He listened to everything Anna had to say the whole time shaking his and blinking rapidly. He threw in the occasional "Oh my God," and "Nooo," as he ran his hands through his hair or threw his arms up in the air. By the time Anna had finished, Steve's complexion was getting close to that of the ghouls who walked the streets.

"So, Logan... Yeah, I guess he's with us now." Steve nodded over and over again.

Anna's smile reached her eyes as she looked at Steve, but he wasn't looking her way. He was too focused on the outside world to notice how much Anna was taken aback. Steve's acceptance of their new addition was lovely, and he never faltered one bit. Logan was just "with us now." Even though the pair of them battled each other often, he was a good guy and a fantastic father. She swallowed the lump in her throat and decided to go check on the children.

Before she reached the door, she said, "I think we need to tell the kids what's going on out there. They must understand what not to do and that they need to obey everything we tell them. They need to know its life and death."

"Ok," Steve paused, staring at the carpet in thought. "Let's go do it now."

"Just give me a minute to try Marcus again; I haven't been able to get a hold of him since it all started," said Anna.

Steve nodded. "Of course... but have you tried Judy's house phone?"

"The line has been playing up all week; she was getting an engineer out Monday morning... tomorrow." Anna shook her head. "But I suppose that won't be happening now."

Steve looked at Anna with sorrow etched into his face. "No, I suppose not."

"You go through, and I'll be there in a minute," she suggested.

Steve went to the children whilst Anna called Marcus's phone again. She listened to the phone's cursed *ring, ring, ring* and began to lose hope that she would ever see him or Judy again. *Surely there's a good explanation for him not having his phone anymore. Marcus is a strong individual; they'll get through this for sure. I've just got to keep the faith.*

* * *

"Aargh!" Rob yelled as the dead man pushed him backwards, trying to grab on to him. Rob managed to get his forearm underneath the creature's chin, pushing its head upwards and teeth away from his face. Having been forced into the bathroom, his hatchet now clattered to the tiled floor.

The dead's arms reached out around Rob, attempting to sink its nails into his flesh and lever its meal towards it. The snapping jaws moved closer and closer. *Ugh, this one smells.*

Rob tried to match its strength for strength, but unfortunately the dead appeared to be far stronger than they were in life. That combined with the surprise attack, and Rob was literally on the back foot.

He tried to scrabble for the knife strapped to his thigh but knew the instant he removed his arm, it would be able to bite him. Rob's legs hit the toilet, and he was forced to sit down on the thing. The toilet seat appeared to be up, too, and he inwardly cringed as his bottom was pushed into the bowl. He had no choice; the thing was driving him downwards. *Can I even fight this one off?*

Rob growled back at the dead man, drawing on all of his reserves but feeling his arms losing strength. He pushed the thing left, crashing into the door, then right towards the bath, hoping to unbalance it. It clung on and continued to push its teeth nearer to Rob's flesh. He could smell a rotting, rancid odour emanating from its open gob and wanted to throw up.

Its face came within three inches of Rob's, and the noises the thing threw out were right inside his earholes now. He twisted away to allow more space between them but also to look around for inspiration. He grunted with the effort, but it became too much. The faces of loved ones began to flash through his mind; his mum, Jack, their grandad, Andy, Anna, and Logan. They flew through his head on a loop as he felt himself about to lose this battle—his life.

That's when the pressure on his arms and body subsided, and the dead man sagged instead. The body was pulled away, replaced by Jack's smiling face in front of him.

"Funny time to take a shit, Rob," Jack said with a smirk on his face.

Rob, panting uncontrollably, looked down at the twice dead

man with Jack's hatchet penetrating the back of its skull. He saw the head of wispy grey hair and realised it was an old guy. *What the fuck!* He began to catch his breath, then dragged his eyes away from the body and looked up at Jack.

"You gonna pull me out or what? I'm jammed in pretty good 'ere," said Rob.

Jack began laughing and couldn't stop. He bent over, howling at Rob's predicament, tears forming in his eyes as he looked back at his older brother.

"Oh, it's like that, is it? You little shithead." The beginnings of a smile started to spread across Rob's face too. "Just get over here and give me a hand before I kick your arse."

"You're not kicking anyone's arse like that." Jack continued laughing but stuck out his hand to pull his brother free. It wasn't so much that he was stuck, more that he had no energy or mental strength left to do it for himself. "Not saying thank you, then?" Jack asked.

"Bugger off," replied Rob.

Rob retrieved his hatchet from the floor. *I should have checked out the other rooms before heading for the closed door.* The bathroom was clearly ok now, but there were two more rooms to view. The small room that he had passed first was easy to see. No corners to hide behind... It was clear.

The next larger room had a bed inside and a massive wardrobe. On closer inspection, Rob realised where the dead guy must've been hidden. There was a gap at the far end of the wardrobe, and the creature must have been behind it somehow. Why on earth it was there was beyond him, though. Rob stared into the space with his face screwed up. *I'm such an idiot.*

That job finished with, he readied himself for the closed door. Although he was reasonably sure there wasn't any

127

danger behind it, he knew he wasn't going to take any chances, either.

"Get ready just in case," Rob said to Jack.

Jack nodded before Rob pushed the handle down, releasing the catch. He pushed the door open fast and wide to throw any possible dangers off guard. There was no movement within the master bedroom, but there was another person in there. Just not one that was a threat.

The little old lady lay on top of the frilly covers with her hands crossed over her chest, clutching a flower. Jack joined Rob by his side, and they both looked down at her with sadness etched onto their faces.

Jack strode over to the bedside table and retrieved an empty pill bottle.

"Do you think these had anything to do with this?" Jack pointed towards the depressing scene in front of them.

Rob raised his eyebrows, assessing the bottle. "Yeah, I reckon so," he said.

"But… why?" Asked Jack.

Rob threw his hands up in the air, looking around the room. "I don't know… maybe her husband, the guy in the bathroom, was scratched, and they knew what was coming to him. So she took some pills and went to sleep before he changed. He must've shut himself out after that."

Rob could see Jack wasn't feeling so happy anymore; he looked downright miserable now. The room was full of memorabilia, old photos, an old fashioned hairbrush on the dressing table, and postcards from long ago. Sorrow started to creep into Rob's soul too.

"Come on, let's leave the lady in peace," said Rob.

Jack nodded and followed his brother down the stairs,

closing the door behind them.

* * *

"I'm going get a few hours' sleep now, Steve," said Anna. "Where's best?"

"You can take my room. If I need any sleep, I'll just nap on the couch," he replied.

"Are you sure? I don't mind the couch."

Steve held up a hand to stop Anna from protesting. "It's fine, honestly, don't worry."

Anna nodded. "Thanks."

"I'll try to get the kids down for a few hours after their tea. Darkness won't be here until after nine anyway, so it'll give them a good start," suggested Steve.

"Yeah, good plan… Maybe you should bring Logan to me when it's time for their sleep."

"Ok."

"Oh, I know we've sorted out the bags that we're taking for the kids, but are you ready to go too? I mean, do you have weapons sorted and some things in a bag… your essentials, et cetera?"

"Yeah, I've got weapons; it's just the thought of having to use them that bothers me. I really don't know how you've done it so far, Anna. I mean, how the hell did you manage to fight those things? I've watched many people try and fail, and I'm seriously worried here," said Steve.

He was looking down at the carpet and rubbing the back of his neck. Anna had never seen him so fragile and unsure of himself. She was torn between enjoying it and feeling sad for him. Ultimately, she needed him to be strong for the kids, all three of them now, so they needed to forget about their petty feuds and start working together.

"Look, Steve, it is not easy out there at all. In fact, it's 100 per cent terrifying. But I know you're exactly like me when it comes to the kids; you'll never give up on them. Alex and Jasper are what got me through those life and death situations. Not once did I worry about my safety; I only worried about not being here for them." Anna stared straight into Steve's eyes now and felt an intensity she never knew she had. "If one of those fuckers runs at you... you smash its head in, or stab it, or throw it, or whatever it is you need to do. And you do it until it stops moving, or it might just end our children's lives. That's all there is to know."

Anna stepped away from Steve to look at him properly. "Get some rest, Steve, because when nightfall comes, it's time to be someone new. You can do it, and so can I, because failing isn't an option."

Anna smiled at Steve, watching him square his shoulders and nod firmly back at her.

"You're right. We can do this... and we will."

* * *

Rob shifted in the armchair he had occupied with his arms crossed over his chest and his feet straight out in front on a footstool. The old people's furniture was surprisingly comfortable even if it was too flowery for his tastes. The curtains had succeeded in keeping most of the daylight out of the small living room allowing Rob a little catch up sleep.

"Rob, are you awake?" asked Jack.

"Well, there's not much chance of being asleep with you talking, is there?" replied Rob.

"I think we should go to Preston... where Anna's going."

Rob blew air out of his nose before answering, "Is that right?"

"Yeah, and I think you do too. You're just too stubborn to admit it," said Jack.

Rob didn't answer.

"Rob?"

"Well, what if they don't make it? Then we turn up at their door, not knowing who we are. It'll be a wasted journey and a risky one," said Rob.

"There's no way Anna isn't gonna make it. Er, hello, have you not met her?" replied Jack.

Rob chuckled to himself. Jack was right, he knew they'd make it there, and he also knew it was his and Jack's best option too. "But what if she's changed her mind and doesn't want us there anymore?"

"Rob... shut up. We're going."

Rob screwed up his eyes. *When the hell did he get so strong-willed and confident?* Jack was leading the way right now, and he was pleased that he was turning into a solid man. *Mum would be so proud.*

"I guess we leave at first dark then," said Rob.

Chapter 16

Anna lay awake for a while before moving. Logan had slept a little, and Anna couldn't help but watch his quiet breaths in and out. *So young and small to lose your parents. I hope he's not too sad. I know the pain all too well, even though I was quite a bit older at fourteen when it happened to me. I at least didn't have a zombie apocalypse to deal with as well.*

She turned away from Logan and stared at the walls instead, thinking of Alex and Jasper now. I'm going to do everything in my power to make sure my kids don't lose me or Steve. But more than anything, they have to survive, so getting them to Preston is paramount. Even if I have to sacrifice myself.

What the hell is going to come of this world now? Will they be able to sort all of this shit out, or are we going to be stuck with a new way of life? Anna rubbed at her eyes, trying to scrub away all the thoughts that swirled around her head. She forced out a breath of air and decided to move.

She joined Steve at the bedroom window to the front of the house. He stood in silence, taking in the outside world with his arms folded and his jaw tense. She followed his gaze and now realised what the noises had been from half an hour earlier. Another house had been penetrated!

The semi-detached houses that lined Steve's street had substantial front windows, allowing an unencumbered view from the sitting room and plenty of light to flood in. However, when the dead roamed the streets and craved live flesh and blood, the windows were no longer appealing.

"The sun is nearly all the way down. Is everything ready to go?" asked Anna as she looked across at him, attempting to gauge his mood.

"Yep," Steve replied without turning his head away from the ongoing horrors of his once peaceful neighbourhood.

"Kids ready?" asked Anna.

"As ready as they can be," replied Steve. "Oh, I've pulled out a crowbar for you in case you wanted to swap the cricket bat over."

Anna nodded. "Thanks, I reckon that will be better." She was about to leave when something occurred to her. "Oh, have you checked the news channels lately?"

"There's nothing on," replied Steve.

"Surely there must be some news on there, can't all be re-runs," asked Anna.

"No, I mean, there's nothing on TV at all. Static only! All transmissions have ceased."

Anna's eyes widened, and her heart picked up its pace. "Holy shit! Are we actually on our own now? Is this it? Is this the end of civilisation as we know it?"

"Who knows?" Steve mumbled, remaining at the window. He'd barely moved in the few minutes Anna had been present, and she understood why now.

She snatched her phone out of her pocket and checked the signal bars at the top of the screen. Four were still present, so Anna hoped it would continue to work for a bit longer.

She thought back to the last news reports from yesterday, wondering if they had decided not to deliver anymore until they had better news to bring. Maybe... Maybe not.

Anna dialled Marcus again, but still nothing. Fuck! She pressed the power button to darken the screen and slipped the phone back into her jeans pocket. Looking back up towards Steve, then out of the window, she could see the last vestiges of light vanishing behind the row of houses in front. Total darkness was probably around ten minutes away.

Gotta keep moving. "We leave in fifteen minutes, Steve." Anna had aimed for a strong voice, but she couldn't help the subdued sounds that left her mouth instead.

* * *

"It's nearly dark," Jack observed, peeking through the side of the curtains.

"Uh-huh," Rob replied.

"Hey, did you notice how much stinkier that guy upstairs is than some of the others this morning," said Jack.

Rob smiled. *Not much escapes his attention.* "I did, especially when the old guy was breathing straight into my mouth."

Jack giggled at this, then said, "Yeah, pretty gross... Do you think they're starting to rot a bit, then? Like normal human bodies would, except without all the walking around and biting people and stuff."

"Maybe... Only time will tell, unfortunately. That is unless the Army actually manages to get off their arses and helps us out a bit." Rob spoke with more venom than he had intended.

What the bloody hell are those guys doing? Probably protecting the capital and leaving the commoners to fend for themselves. Absolute joke the Armed Forces are nowadays. Glad I got out just in time.

Rob looked up from checking his backpack to see Jack observing him. His face must have painted his frustrations, because Jack didn't ask a single question.

"You nearly ready?" asked Rob in his usual curt manner.

"Always ready, bro," replied Jack brimming with energy and throwing Rob a big grin.

"Ok, then," said Rob, returning the grin, but it didn't quite reach his eyes. His thoughts were entirely on Anna and what she was doing.

* * *

Anna looked down at the kids standing near the patio doors, ready to go. They had their lightweight jackets on, zipped up to the top, with Logan still wearing his from earlier. All three looked up to Anna with eyes the size of saucers and their mouths zipped shut. *This is so hard.* The talk had gone very well, but Anna hoped they understood the situation's gravity outside. A tiny bit of her also hoped they hadn't and could stay children for many more years yet. *God, I hate this.*

Steve joined them all there and said, "Just found this wind-up radio—might come in handy."

"Not if there's no one there to broadcast," replied Anna, wishing she hadn't as Alex's big brown eyes locked on to her own hazel ones. Anna reached out and stroked her daughter's cheek, attempting to wipe away any fears she might be feeling. Anna knew it was futile, but she would also never give up where her children were concerned.

Steve put the small radio into his backpack and nodded to Anna he was ready. He crouched down to speak to the kids on their level. "Right, little people, do we know the plan?"

All three nodded in silence, the way they had been instructed to do. No talking, no noises, and everybody stick together. Steve's eyes found Anna's, reflecting her own insecurities in that one look. *Oh God, are we doing the right thing dragging our children out into this shitty world?*

"Ok… time to go," Anna said.

Steve stared at her with his eyes wider than she had ever seen them. She felt the same way, especially because she had been out there and faced the horrors. Now she was asking her children to do the same—and Steve, come to think of it.

"Stay here whilst I check the other side of the fence," said Anna.

Anna eased the curtain back, avoiding the scraping metal sound that curtain poles could produce. Next, she coaxed open the patio door and stepped out into the much cooler air than she had experienced that morning. The silence was eerie as she crept to the back fence, checking left and right into the neighbouring gardens.

Anna collected the small step ladders that Steve had stored behind the shed and set them up, trying not to clatter the metal. Once on top, she could see a small portion of the path through the foliage, so she climbed over to view the whole area before allowing the kids out.

Anna made her way through the trees and bushes, then reached around to her backpack and gripped the crowbar protruding from it. Keeping her hand attached to its shaft, she rotated her head left whilst craning farther out into the open. She stared at the empty expanse of the track for a full ten seconds, watching for any signs of movement and listening out for growls or footsteps, before repeating the process to the right.

Satisfied there wasn't anything left, right, or on the path near Steve's back garden, Anna sneaked back to the fence and signalled to Steve using her hand. She could hear the kids shuffling towards her, and she had to stifle a sob. Her heart pounded through her chest for the hundredth time that day, but this felt so much worse. Her babies were heading out into the darkness because she had told them to.

Get a fucking grip, Anna. You're no use to them scared out of your wits. Anna had to shake her head hard to fire herself up in the right way. *No more pity... No more fear... Only fire and strength.* Anna clenched her teeth and dug her fingernails into her palms, readying herself for the most incredible fight of her life.

* * *

"We'll use the garden fences again to get us back out onto that main road, and hopefully it'll be clear of the dead. Fingers crossed, we can get off of these housing estates. After that, it should be plain sailing," said Rob.

"Got it," Jack issued a thumbs up at the same time.

Rob checked the back way was still clear before opening the curtains, then he slid the door back open and stepped out into the night. His hand was resting on his hatchet whilst he beckoned for Jack to follow. Rob tilted his head, hearing the unending choir of the demons still outside his friends' house. He could hear nothing closer, though, so they proceeded to traverse the gardens in the opposite direction from which they had come.

It didn't take them long before they were nearing the bigger road. The cul-de-sac nearest to them had a fence cutting off the more prominent street, and Rob decided it might be an excellent place to view it. Once they entered, they would be in full view of the monstrous creatures out there. There were odd trees to hide behind, but Rob didn't fancy getting trapped, so he took a few moments to assess the street scene first.

* * *

Steve lifted the kids over the fence one at a time to Anna, who placed them on the ground at her side. Each time, she lowered her face to theirs and pressed her index finger to her lips, watching for their understanding.

All three kids were now over, so she slid back out of the bushes to recheck the area as Steve clambered over the fence. They were still clear. She rotated her head to check Steve was watching her and signalled them all forwards onto the pathway. *This is it.*

Anna grabbed the nearest child's hand, Jasper, and stealthily jogged in the right direction. Steve brought up the rear, clutching Alex's and Logan's hands with death grips. He, too, had his crowbar sticking out of the top of his backpack, ready to go in an instant; Anna had made sure of it.

The children all looked around, trying to catch the smallest of movements, per Anna's instructions. They could provide early warnings for things the adults might not see. It was their way to contribute too. When Anna had addressed the children and suggested this idea, Alex was straight on it. Anna knew she wanted to help protect the younger ones, proving she was a big girl now. *My big girl.*

They made it the two hundred metres to where the track crossed the road. Anna had them all squat behind a large group of bushes whilst she eyed the space they needed to travel through next.

Steve studied the area behind them. There was a line of trees around one hundred and fifty metres away, so Anna signalled to move forwards again. They scurried along the footpaths, staying close to the fences that separated this road from the nearby streets before taking cover behind two large trees.

Nothing moved, besides the leaves on the trees as Anna tried to concentrate on the surrounding area. Her children were close behind her making everything so much worse. She wanted and needed them close, but being out here with them terrified her to her core. Their jackets rustled way too loudly. They breathed and coughed and sniffled all the time. And more than anything her blood pounded in her ears reminding her of how panicked she still was.

Anna shook off the terror and began to step out from behind their cover. She stopped dead in her tracks when her eyes locked onto a zombie very close to where they were stood. Holding her breath, she returned to her position behind the tree, and held out her palm towards Steve and the kids. The beast was wandering and hadn't yet clocked them. *It's only a matter of time before it sees us. Shit. If I was on my own, I'd just stay hidden in this bush, but I can't risk it with the kids.*

It was ambling without purpose, and Anna inwardly cursed again, realising it was shuffling closer to their position. If it found them, it might let out one of its shrieks or growls, alerting more demons to the possibility of fresh meat. *Shit, shit, shit.* Anna dragged her eyes away from the dead thing, turning to see her children instead. *Time to be strong, Anna.*

Chapter 17

Anna lifted her finger to her mouth, eyeballing Steve, and indicated they should stay there. She had hoped they wouldn't come across any of the dead so soon, but she knew she had to act; there was no choice. Her hand reached back to the crowbar and pulled its long metal shaft free, feeling its coolness against her palm. She shifted the grip of it in her hand to hold the straight end whilst staring at the creature.

The streetlight nearby illuminated long brown hair, belonging to what used to be a woman. There was no mistaking the persistent guttural noises it continued to produce, though. It turned its back to them briefly. *This is it; this is the moment to pounce.*

She covered the three metres like a sprinter, but with deadly silence. The only sound to be heard was the whipping noise from the crowbar tearing at the monsters head. The blow was devastating; Anna had swung it from right to left, hitting its temple. *Fuck, was that too loud?*

The beast crumpled to the ground. Anna couldn't believe she had floored it with only one strike. She stared at it for a moment, making sure it remained downed, poised to strike again and again if need be like she had done with the cricket bat. She examined the crowbar with awe before realising she should get her arse out of sight and hauled it back over to the group's hiding spot.

Steve looked at Anna open-mouthed. He craned his head around her to check out the dead zombie again before whispering, "Holy shit!"

Anna displayed her hands in front of her and shrugged. "The crowbar works well."

"Noted," whispered Steve.

Anna looked around again for another twenty seconds before she motioned for them all to move to the next safe place to take cover. *God, I hate being out here with my kids. Am I a bad mother for doing this? I know I often think I'm a bad mother for silly things like forgetting the £1 they need to buy a raffle strip at school, or not taking them out places more, but this is entirely different. This could get them all killed.* Anna tried to shake away the self-doubt and concentrate on what she was doing. They moved along this street, and Anna started feeling a little hopeful at the lack of the dead. *Don't get complacent, it could all change in a heartbeat.*

They scurried along an expanse of the open footpath, heading towards a small section of bushes. Anna was holding Alex's hand firmly, with the crowbar in her other hand, whilst Steve held the boys' hands. They reached the farthest point of the bush they were hiding behind when Anna looked back to Steve and the boys, checking they were still close.

"ANNA!" shouted Steve.

Anna's head spun in Alex's direction, just about to witness her daughter's face being bitten. It had its bony hands locked onto her shoulders and was nearing her face with its chomping jaw. Anna's left hand yanked Alex back in a reflex action that had her daughter flinging away from the dead. It was pulled along with her, though, so Anna stuck her foot into the beast's side, dislodging it from Alex.

Anna jerked Alex farther away, not caring how she landed, just so that she was away from the dead. She chased the zombie that had stumbled away and kicked at it again, this time sending it sprawling on the ground. Anna's face contorted into a snarl, filled with rage and hatred. She ran up to its head and kicked with a force she had never known possible, hearing a crack coming from its neck. The bastard thing still moved, so Anna brought her crowbar down onto its face, beating it wide open until it did stop moving. *Dirty fucker!*

Anna tried to contain her breathing but realised they may have drawn more of the dead to their location. She scanned the area, seeing Steve holding Alex tight whilst she sobbed into his shirt. *Dear God, I nearly lost my child. Stay focused, Anna. Keep your fucking eyes open. Too much thinking about being a bad mother and you've become one.*

Anna went over to Alex, kneeling down to hug her. She wrapped her arms around her little girl and had to fight to keep the tears out of her eyes. She breathed in her coconut shampoo whilst she continued her scanning of the surrounding area. Her daughter's tears touched Anna's face, feeling cold, and it pained her so much she didn't know what to do.

"I'm here, sweetie, don't you worry. We'll be fine, I promise," said Anna, cringing at the blatant lie. It was something that couldn't be promised, but to a child, it meant the world.

"Steve, let's carry on and get us all to safety," said Anna, jaw set.

Steve rubbed at his temples, adding a slow nod afterwards.

It wasn't going to be all plain sailing, but they had no choice; they had to get there.

They managed to cover a mile in Anna's estimation. Every step forwards meant one step closer to safety. They were crouched behind the hedgerow of a large house when an alarming collaboration of sounds was carried to their ears. Steve's head popped up like that of a meerkat before spinning in Anna's direction. Disturbing wails of possibly several humans aligned with the growls Anna had come to know all too well.

"That sounded pretty close, Anna," said Steve, attempting to keep his voice calm but failing.

Anna nodded her response, contemplating their next move. Her eyes fell on the three children once more, who had been incredible so far. But Anna knew if they were to be chased by many creatures at once, there was a good chance they wouldn't make it.

She shuffled towards the opening of the driveway and surveyed the road they still had to travel. There was a car with its front doors open a crack.

"Steve, check out this car just up the road. Do you reckon you could hot-wire it?" asked Anna, wondering how far Steve's car knowledge stretched.

Steve shuffled forwards to join Anna and view the car she was talking about. The mere fact that Steve never denied being able to hot-wire cars was encouraging.

"It's an older model, so maybe I could. There's always the chance of an alarm going off, though, and clearly we don't want that," he replied.

"No… we do not," said Anna, biting her lip.

A plan began to form in her head, should an alarm occur, and she was sure that this would be their best option. She dragged her palms down her face and nodded to herself, knowing they had to do this.

Steve sniffed the air audibly, and Anna joined in, noticing the new tang to the environment. "Fire. I wonder how close?"

BOOM!

All five of them jumped heavenward as the loud noise rang out from not very far away. It drowned out the growls that were still lingering in the air just moments before and shook every one of them to their cores.

"Shit!" mumbled Steve, shuffling back to the kids, who had trembling lips, eyes darting in all directions and had let several whimpers escape their tiny mouths. Anna did the same, holding Alex and Logan close to her body. She saw Jasper clutching on to Steve like a vice and decided they had to make a move and fast. *It's getting worse out here.*

Anna addressed them all, "Kids, you've got to be brave now and very quiet. Can you guys do it?"

Alex, Logan, and Jasper weren't as enthusiastic with their agreement this time around. Still, Anna hoped they could manage just a bit longer. She rechecked the street and indicated they all should follow her.

They shuffled towards the car, hugging the hedges and walls of nearby gardens and reached it within just a minute and a half. Anna directed them behind another nearby hedge and sent Steve to go check out the car.

* * *

Right... Ok... Here's your chance to contribute, Steve. Just don't fuck it up! Steve darted towards the older model Toyota Corolla. It had been a long time since he had played around with cars, so he hoped his mind would bring back the details he so badly needed.

The internet would be a great help right now. He decided against using his phone in this deadly environment. The screen would be too bright, and he wouldn't be able to play any videos out loud, anyway. *Just concentrate!*

Steve reached the car with his heart thudding in his eardrums. He twisted his head from side to side, almost too quickly to take in his surroundings. It appeared they were still alone on this street, so he opened the front passenger door wide enough to crawl into the car.

Creak...

The groaning of metal echoed through the quiet street.

Nooo! You fucking idiot, you know older cars do that. Steve's heart rate sped up tenfold as he shot terrified glances all around. He didn't know what to do next, continue into the car or keep watching for anything coming at him.

He pulled the crowbar free and stood up to peer over the car roof with a grimace on his face. His hearing was impaired because his damned heartbeat wouldn't shut the hell up. *For God's sake, man up, Steve*, he berated himself, clutching the crowbar and turning his head and body a full 360 degrees.

Steve's eyes widened when his ears picked up noises from 4 o'clock to his location. Running feet and tortured growls closed in on him as the world slowed down. He had to drag himself in the direction of the noise, unable to move. When he did, his eyes locked on to the beast, who was lit up beneath the street light there.

146

Steve managed to haul his body around to face the beast squarely, and not for one second did he contemplate running. *My kids need this car; I'm not running away from it and them.* The monster was three or four steps away from him now. He managed one step towards it, only able to raise the crowbar into a defensive position.

Steve's eyes focused on the creature's widening mouth, displaying teeth and darkness. It flew through the air at Steve, who brought up the crowbar just below its face. The momentum of the charging beast forced them both to the ground with the deadly thing on top.

The noise emanating from its throat was relentless and ear-splitting so close up. Steve became aware of his backpack's contents, they were digging into his back whilst he pushed at the thing with his weapon. He could feel its strength bearing down on him and its iron grip on his arms. *Fuck you!* Steve growled right back at it and rolled the two of them over, so he was now straddling the beast with the crowbar still pushing at its chest and neck.

CRUNCH! A crowbar was rammed through its eyeball and straight through its useless brain, hitting the harder skull at the back and cracking the bone there.

Steve blinked several times, trying to comprehend what had just happened, then followed the crowbar's shaft to see Anna standing over the two of them.

Anna yanked her weapon back out, causing a sucking noise and casting stringy gore everywhere. Steve could barely contain his gag reflex seeing a few droplets of congealing blood splatter on his jacket. He looked down, trying to decide if it was brain matter or pieces of eyeball making their way down his front.

"You good?" Anna asked with intensity as her eyes darted around. Steve looked back up at Anna. *Who the fuck are you now?* He made a mental note never to piss Anna off again and nodded, more to himself than Anna.

"Ok, good, but you need to move now," said Anna.

Steve jumped off the double dead person and evaluated the area once more before climbing into the vehicle. He spread himself across the front seats, attempting to locate where to pull the wires from when something glinting on the floor caught his eye. The glow of the streetlights added illumination to the vehicle's interior, and Steve blew out a relieved breath, realising what he was looking at.

"Keys! You absolute beauty."

Finding the correct key, he pushed it into the ignition and left it there a second whilst he signalled to Anna. Having returned to the children on the other side of the hedgerow, she did a quick left and right of the street and ushered them forwards to the car.

Steve climbed into the driver's seat, readying for the right moment to turn the key. He had seen too many times now how fast things could go downhill once that engine came to life. He scanned the surrounding area all whilst Anna opened the rear door and helped them in.

"Get in the footwells, kids, and don't come up until I tell you to," said Steve, watching them clambering in and down to hide.

He continued to scour the trees and houses nearby and the adjoining streets. The side they had come from had fewer side streets than the opposite, but he could only see so far down because of the car's position.

Tree branches moved, and his heart caught in his throat.

Nothing... It was nothing. Steve watched Anna in the wing mirror close the back door with her hip to stifle any sound. The car rocked from this action, and Steve remembered he was still wearing his backpack. He was feeling a little constricted and wondered if he could drive ok with it on. However, he was uncertain about removing it if they had to make a swift exit.

Anna stepped towards the front door and placed her hand on it before stopping and said, "Steve, start the engine now."

Steve tried the ignition but nothing; he frantically checked the dashboard; some of the lights had lit up, but the stupid thing had not started. *The battery must be ok; otherwise, there'd be nothing, surely.* He knew that wasn't true; a struggling battery could still light up the dashboard and not start the car.

Please start, please start. He could see Anna staring at him but did not return the look; instead, he tried the key again, which threw noises out of the car—turning over noises, but still not catching and firing up. *No, you fucking piece of shit... WORK.* Steve jammed his foot onto the accelerator and twisted the key.

VRRUUMM! The engine choked to life.

Grinning with utter hysteria, he looked at Anna and could see she was looking towards a side street opposite but farther back from the car. He pivoted his head round to see three, then four, then eight pairs of feet thundering around the corner straight towards them. He knew they would be on them in a matter of seconds.

He was about to scream at Anna, but she beat him to it. "DRRIIVVEE!" She slammed the door and raced away from the car, heading straight for the beasts.

Chapter 18

NOOO! Steve's mind yelled at him. The kids screamed too, forcing him into action.

He looked forwards where more beasts were running at them from around the corner of the side street in front. He rammed the gear stick into first as muscle memory had his body doing all the right things quicker than ever. His foot hit the accelerator, the car sped forward, and he allowed first gear to whine, pushing the rpm to its limit.

Second gear, and the beasts were nearly on them. He mounted the nearside curb, veering away from the crowd racing towards them. *THUD! THUD!* The dead things bodies were hitting the metal of the car. Two of the dead attacked the rear of the car whilst he continued to build speed. He moved a little farther ahead when a creature pinged off the front bumper.

Third gear, and they were nearly away from the crowd when a lone beast launched itself from the left. It must have been in one of those gardens and heard the advancing car and group of adoring fans. Its head struck the windshield making the kids cry out at the loud crack that rang out through the interior of the vehicle.

It tried to cling on, not having done enough damage to its head. Steve swerved the car and the creature to the left and scraped them along the brick wall that had emerged. The dead thing barely registered that its lower half was being crushed. Still, the car's sheer force and the wall eventually dragged it from the vehicle's bonnet. Thudding and scraping noises joined the scream of the car's engine.

Steve straightened up the car on the road again and checked for any more movement up ahead. When he was sure there was no immediate danger, he chanced a look in the rear-view mirror, knowing full well he would be too far away now to spot Anna. He could only see their pursuers, reducing in size and menace. He sped down the road, moving into the right gears for their speed, heading towards Preston and hopefully their safety.

* * *

Anna sprinted towards the dead, hoping she could make the gap that was shrinking by the second. This had been her plan B all along. If the time came to help her children get to safety, she would run and take the dead with her. Steve would get the kids out of here now; cars were his thing and those were the skills he possessed. Anna's was her ability to run, so run she must.

She pushed her body forward. It was crazy to be running straight at these things. *Surely only love could make a person be this mental.*

Her breathing was louder than the creatures' growls, and

she could still smell the burning scent when she sucked more air into her lungs. Her boots pounding on the road added to the pounding feet of the dead pursuing her.

The streetlights bounced off the heads of the charging herd. Anna lengthened her stride, aiming for the dwindling hole up front. Three beasts were a little ahead of the mob, so she pulled the crowbar from her bag, gripping it in two hands to not hinder her running.

She closed the gap and knew this was it; they were here, almost close enough to breathe on her. The whining sound of a straining engine became clear, and she hoped to God they were going to make it. She dared not look behind her as the first beast reached out its monstrous fingers and brushed the sleeve of her leather jacket. The scraping sound felt like it crawled over her flesh too.

The second beast stepped in front of her just off to the left, so Anna dipped her shoulder and barged into its chest, sending it soaring backwards. The hit had slowed Anna a tad when another monster stepped in front. She pulled the crowbar back and let it swing at the thing's head with a scathing crack. Not a killing blow, but enough to shove it away from her path.

Anna allowed her stride to stretch out once more, noticing the car's noise getting louder but farther away at the same time. Her body worked in perfect synchronicity, legs and arms pumping away to give her the speed she needed. The pounding of her own feet on the ground carried up through her body, and she took pleasure in it. She took another four long paces before allowing herself a look over her shoulder.

The car was currently mounting the curb, avoiding an advancing crowd. *They must be from the other street. Fuck!* Most of the beasts from this street were following her, though—live prey. She spun her head forwards again, thinking. *Come on, Steve, get your foot down.*

Anna progressed down the street a little farther away from her chasers, throwing another glance over her shoulder. She could hardly hear the car now, just the angry wails of the monsters wanting her body. But she could see the car up the road, the other side of their crowd of demons, She wouldn't allow herself to believe they were safe yet, not until she saw it with her own eyes. *If I survive this, that is.*

* * *

"I can smell whatever it was that went boom. Can't you, Rob?" asked Jack, sniffing the air and viewing the cul-de-sac in front of him.

"Yeah, it's gotta be a car, I reckon; not many things could go up like that," replied Rob, peering over the fence.

They were right on top of the main road now, and Rob was assessing their chances. He swivelled his head from left to right, not seeing anything at all. He was about to signal the all-clear to Jack when his ears picked up something on the night air.

The thunderous noise of pounding feet and the growls of the dead broached the relative quietness of the cul-de-sac. *They must be chasing some poor fool.*

Jack jumped up to join Rob on the fence, saying, "That sounds just like when I helped Anna. They must be chasing someone, and it sounds like there're loads of 'em too."

Rob was about to step down away from the fence when he

decided against it. He scrunched his eyes closed, attempting to shake the nagging feeling away. If there was someone out there that they could help without putting themselves at too much risk, then they should. They wouldn't have met Anna if Jack had ignored her plight, which meant Logan would be dead too.

Rob opened his eyes to see what was going on when Jack said, "Hey, that's a woman running towards us!"

Rob's head flew towards where Jack pointed, and straight afterwards, his eyes widened in horror. "Anna!" Rob said, clutching the fence tighter. There was no mistaking her leather jacket and blonde ponytail bobbing around in the gentle glow of the streetlights. It was her, alright.

"Shiiittt, does she go around looking for hoards to chase her?" Jack asked, head swivelling between the advancing crowd and Rob's face.

"Jack, jump down behind me and hold on to my body." He looked down at Jack's face and emphasised the words when he said, "*You need to hold me tight.*"

"Ok," agreed Jack.

Rob's head popped back over the top of the fence as Anna and the crowd were almost on them.

"ANNA!" Rob yelled in her direction, hoping she could see him as well as he could see her.

Her head was twisting from side to side, searching for the source of the voice. Rob waved his arms in the air until she finally understood where he was.

"OVER HERE, ANNA!" Rob shouted once more, then did a quick check over his shoulder and said to Jack, "Keep a lookout for anything our side."

Anna was maybe ten paces away now, so Rob leant over the

six-foot fence and held out his right arm, ready to drag her over to their side. Rob waited for Anna to reach him. *How has she come to be running from so many again? And where the hell is her family?*

* * *

Anna had a few more strides to go before she reached the six-foot fence. She could see Rob leaning far over it, reaching out his arm, ready for her to take it and be hoisted to some level of safety. *How on earth have they found me again?*

Anna ran, realising she was still holding the crowbar in her hands; she knew she would need both of them free. She pushed the long crowbar through her belt loop, just managing it before she reached Rob and the fence.

A hurried check behind her; she had a good few seconds lead on the things to clamber up and over. *This is it, Anna, time it right.* She reached out her right hand whilst adjusting her footing to do this in one fluid motion.

Anna's forearm hit Rob's hand as she grasped his muscular arm; she was then lifted off the ground and allowed her momentum to assist. She threw her left leg up towards the top of the fence whilst Rob swung her up and towards safety. Her leg hooked over the top, at the same time his other hand grabbed her arse, manhandling her upwards.

Jack helped her clamber down as the first of the thuds hit the wooden planks from the other side. Anna jumped, and so did Jack. They scurried farther away from it should the inevitable happen and the dead burst through the fence. *Holy shit, that was close.*

Rob jumped down next to them, grabbing Anna's hand. He dragged her away. "Come on, we've gotta get out of here."

A lone beast charged at them when they faced away from the fence. Jack was nearest to it, so he pulled his hatchet from his hip and swung at its face as if he'd done it a thousand times before. The weapon struck through the temple and eye socket, and the beast fell to the ground. Jack appeared calm as he pulled the hatchet free from the dead woman, using his foot on her face. He wiped it clean on her clothes, much the way his brother had done previously. *Jack seems to be adapting to this shit pretty well.*

The three then ran towards the third semi-detached house down the street and headed straight for its back garden. Rob gripped the clasp of the gate, finding it unlocked. They ran straight on through into the garden, then closed the gate behind them and slid the bolt across.

They marched across the grass, dodging the various toys strewn about, and headed for the neighbouring fence. Anna looked across towards the house, registering its curtains were shut, so maybe the family still hid inside. She looked down at the ground to the Little Tikes car and scooter abandoned there, and her breath caught in her throat.

Emotions began to build within her, thinking of her children and Logan, then the possible children inside this house. *What is to become of them all? How are they going to survive this horror show?*

Rob's hand squeezed hers, and she realised he hadn't yet let it go. It was rough, warm, and felt so strong; something she needed right now. She dragged her eyes away from the colourful plastic and saw Rob looking at her.

"We need to move, Anna. Over the garden fences will keep us safer to move across the estate," said Rob in a calm voice.

Anna nodded back to him and touched her locket. Her children, her world, her reason for being. Jack began climbing into the next garden, and Anna and Rob followed.

Chapter 19

Anna, Rob, and Jack travelled across the housing estate in silence, choosing when to remain hidden in gardens and when to make a dash for the next spot. The night had barely begun and neither had their journey, but Anna felt with every step that she was just a tiny bit closer to her children and knowing if they'd made it or not.

Anna gasped suddenly. *I can call Steve's parents' house to see if they made it there.* She couldn't phone Steve in case they needed to be silent, but she could call his parents.

She pulled the phone from her zipped-up pocket and reached for the power on button before stopping herself. In her haste to find out about the kids, she forgot that she, Rob, and Jack needed to be quiet too, and her stupid phone made a loud tune whilst turning on. She may as well stand in the middle of the street screaming.

"Shit," Anna whispered to herself.

"What's up?" asked Rob.

"I wanted to call Steve's parents' house to see if they got there, but daren't turn on my phone out here," she replied.

The three of them were squatting in some large bushes of a garden that was quite overgrown. It was tricky manoeuvring around the foliage, but it certainly gave good cover. Rob crouch-walked from under the bushes and began looking around at the other houses and gardens before returning to Jack and Anna's position.

"I reckon we're not too far away from this estate opening up onto the country roads; maybe we can find a house to take cover in and make that phone call," Rob suggested.

Anna bolted upright. "Hang on a minute, whereabouts are we... I mean, what street?"

"Not sure what the street is, but I'm certain we're near Thanet Primary School," replied Rob.

"Oh shit, that's right near my Aunt's house. My Aunt Judy and cousin, Marcus."

Rob nodded. "Ok, have a look and see if you know where to go from here."

Anna recognised that they were only a couple of streets over. They clambered over the few remaining garden fences and scurried down the street to get to the right house. It was harder to take cover down this particular road; not many shrubs or trees, and all the places had open front windows like that of Steve's.

They got close enough to see Judy's house in the dark. Anna sucked in a breath and had to hold back tears. Rob followed Anna's gaze, then turned back to her, dragging her away from the wide-open street and around a safer corner. Jack followed as they all hid for a moment down the side of a house, squatting behind their wheelie bins and breathing in the disgusting odour.

Anna closed her eyes, seeing the carnage once again... The smashed front window, the wide open front door... It looked like it had been broken and pushed inwards. The beautiful

159

floral curtains Anna had helped Judy pick out were now flapping through the broken window. They were torn at the bottom, and the curtain pole had been pulled from the wall too.

"Oh God, they must be dead," whispered Anna, touching her locket.

Rob crouched closer to her. "Well, looking at the scene, the house has been penetrated, but no zombies are floating about, either. I've seen houses that have been attacked and the dead stick around for quite a while afterwards. In my mind, the only reason the zombies might not be there anymore is if they chased someone away. Do you think Marcus and Judy could run like you can?"

Anna considered what Rob was saying, and a tiny flicker of hope entered her thoughts. "Marcus could; we ran together sometimes. If anything, I'd say he's faster and stronger than me." Anna looked down towards the floor, contemplating her words. "But Judy... I... I don't think she could at all."

Anna slowly shook her head, allowing the tears to fall. There were two sets of hands-on her back now, rubbing and patting. She sniffed before adding, "Judy needed a walking stick sometimes and struggled with the stairs occasionally. Oh God... I dread to think what might have happened to her in her last moments."

"You don't know that's what happened in there; maybe we should go in and look. Me and Rob?" Jack suggested, looking as sad as she felt.

"I'll go take a look. Jack, you stay here with Anna so she's not alone."

Jack nodded and moved slightly closer to Anna. Rob checked the street for any movement before darting across it towards the house.

* * *

Rob stepped over the threshold, carefully placing one boot, then the next, trying not to disturb any broken glass. He moved through the house, eyes darting left and right, then looked up the stairs.

He slid his hatchet from its holster, feeling its familiar weight in the palm of his hand and readying himself, should he need to fight. He moved towards the front room doorway and peered around the corner.

He could see the destroyed window and torn curtains, then moved his head to take in the rest of the living room. The room was empty, with furniture upturned and ornaments flung around and smashed.

He followed the hallway to the back of the house and entered the kitchen. The patio doors were still closed with the curtain pulled across, and most things were still in one piece in here. Even in the dark, Rob could see it was a homely kitchen, just like that of his mum.

Thud.

Rob spun and faced the direction of the noise; at the same time, a beast hurled itself at him. He managed to get his arms up between the two of them but was pushed backwards and tripped over a chair leg, smashing into the kitchen bin. Something pierced his flesh in the back of his thigh, and pain tore through his leg. *Please don't let that be the zombie virus inside me.* He continued to force the creature away from himself,

161

determined not to make the same mistake as last time.

Rob pushed and rolled, gaining the upper hand by straddling the beast. He held the creature with his left arm and body and, whipping the hatchet back, drove it forwards into the zombie's skull. It instantly stopped moving! Rob closed his eyes and sucked in huge a lungful of air. *Why does this keep happening to me?*

He brushed himself off, noticing the bin that had been smashed when he landed on it. There were shards of plastic everywhere, with one piece in particular half covered in blood. *That's what stabbed me... Thank God.*

He found a tea towel hanging on the radiator and used it to tie around his leg, stemming the bleeding. The blood looked to be slowing down, so it must have been a shallow wound. He breathed out a loud and long breath. *Keep moving, Rob.*

He shook away any thoughts he didn't need right now and concentrated on being vigilant and sharp. He crept up the stairs, noticing photos smashed on the carpet and flung all around. He couldn't see who was in them, but he could guess that Anna was in a fair few. Glass crunched underfoot as he took the steps at a slow pace.

He reached the top, and there was a dead body visible on the back bedroom floor. Before entering, he assessed the rest of the upstairs from where he was standing. If there was anything else in this house that wanted to eat him, surely it would have made itself known by now.

He stepped into the room. It was brighter than the rest of the house as the curtains were pulled back, and the nearby streetlight flooded in. The window was wide open, creating a gap large enough that a man could climb through. The body he stepped over was that of a young woman, twice dead. Her head was caved in, making her face unrecognisable.

After dodging two more dead beasts, he reached the window and looked through the open frame without overexposing himself. He took in the grassed garden and pretty flower beds and knew if it was him in this house under attack, he could easily jump from this window. He looked farther out and noticed a smashed wooden table just below the window and a wandering zombie within the garden too. *How did that get in there? The gate is closed and there are no breaks in the fence. Very odd.*

Rob retreated from the room and its stench. After viewing the bathroom, he went to the only other bedroom up there. The door was closed, so he listened the same way he had in the last house. At least this time, he knew the rest of the house was empty. *I bloody hope.*

He charged into the room, brandishing his hatchet, only to realise there was a similar body to the old lady he had seen earlier that day. A smallish red-headed lady lay on the bed like she was sleeping. She had a bottle of pills in her hand. *What the hell is it with pills today?* Sadness washed over him. If she was anything like Anna, he imagined she would have been a lovely lady to know.

Rob sat next to the lady he assumed was Judy and attempted to understand what might have happened here. The room looked untouched by the dead, so she must have done this before they got into the house. Maybe they had been surrounded, and she decided to end it all, freeing Marcus to make a run for it. *Maybe. That would make her a good woman too. Selfless.*

Rob made his way back across the street to Anna and Jack. "Come on, let's get into one of these houses and then you can make your phone call. I'll tell you all about inside your Aunt's

163

once we're off the street," he said, stroking Anna's cheek and gazing into her glassy eyes.

* * *

Rob gained easy access to the house opposite Judy's, which looked to be empty with its curtains wide open. Anna closed the downstairs curtains, shielding herself from the image across the street and the three of them from being seen by the dead. Once they were protected, Anna removed her phone and powered it on, waiting for it to come to life whilst she bounced on the balls of her feet.

She paced the small sitting room, holding her phone out in front of her, watching the various stages of preparing itself for use. Anna stared at the screen, waiting for the signal icon to pop up, but it never did; the red circle with a diagonal line through it appeared instead.

"No…" It came out more of a sound on her breath than a word.

She checked around the room for a landline telephone, finding one in the corner. She snatched the handset up and held it to her ear, listening for a dial tone. There was nothing there either, just silence. *Why?*

Jack and Rob returned to the sitting room and looked at her with concerned expressions. Anna held out the handset and said, "There's no signal on the mobile and no dial tone on the landline either… I mean… what the fuck! How could it all have vanished so fucking quickly?"

"Shit," replied Rob, taking the handset from Anna and trying it himself.

"I expected the mobile network to drop fast, but I'm surprised at the landline... I wonder if the cables in the area have been compromised in some way?" Jack said, screwing up his face like he was concentrating hard.

"So maybe they're working elsewhere, just not here?" replied Anna.

"Maybe?" suggested Jack. "It's not a certainty, though. There could be something else bigger going on stopping landlines in all of Hull or all of the UK for all I know. But I am surprised."

"So we need to find another house with a landline... Let's go," said Anna, picking up her pack.

"Erm... ok. We need to check first, though, right?" Rob said, eyeing Anna and nodding. "Right?"

"No, we should just go. It was clear a few moments ago," replied Anna.

"Oh, come on, Anna," Rob said gently. "You don't know that the phones will even work in another house. We always have to check first... you know that."

Anna sighed, knowing full well she was being rash and needed to calm herself down a tad. She was unravelling and had to keep it together if she was to survive this night. And she didn't want to risk Jack and Rob's lives just so she could find another phone. *Not cool, Anna.*

"We will get to your children, Anna, I know we will. And I'm damn sure they're all ok... I just feel it. You getting your knickers in a twist isn't going to change what's already happened or not happened. For their sake, you need to keep your head straight so we can all get there safely," said Rob.

Anna looked from Rob to Jack, then back to Rob, feeling like a lunatic. *Why am I such a control freak?* "Sorry, yeah. You're right."

"Right…" Rob said. "Ok, just give us few minutes and we'll—"

"HELP! HELP!" *BANG! BANG! BANG!* "Please help me!" *BANG! BANG! BANG!*

The voice and banging were coming from just outside. Rob and Jack rushed upstairs, with Anna following behind. All three of them huddled around the edges of the curtains, peeking out onto the street.

A woman was running from door to door, banging and screaming like no one could hear her, even the zombies. She was just a few doors away from their commandeered house, and if she didn't shut up—like *now*—she would be bringing trouble onto herself and them too.

Chapter 20

"We've gotta help her!" Jack said far too loud.

Rob's hand darted out when Jack attempted to dash past him; Rob said, "No, Jack, it's already too late."

"What? Don't be stupid; we can help her," replied Jack.

Jack started to move back towards the window again when a blood-curdling scream let rip just below. There was a kind of rumbling noise, too, followed by a cacophony of growls.

Anna's eye's had barely left the street this whole time, watching the woman trying to get help. The beasts were on her too fast, and by the time they had seen her, they would never have been able to help. More and more of the dead flooded the street, having heard the poor woman's frantic and reckless cries.

Anna looked on, not able to tear her eyes from the horrific scene. The woman was pulled apart by the wicked things attacking her. They tore into her flesh with their teeth and somehow managed to pull her arm and leg off as they fought over her limbs. They clambered over each other, desperate to sink their teeth into her body, to taste her blood. *Dear God, when they're finished with the poor woman, there'll be nothing left to become one of them.* The screaming carried on for a few seconds after too. She was still alive as they ate and pulled her limbs off.

"Shit!" Rob said, pulling away from the curtain and leaving the room.

Anna felt the same; they never stood a chance of helping her. But they were also now stuck in this house and having to remain quiet—for the time being, anyway. She and Jack followed Rob down the stairs, as she still had to find out about Judy and Marcus.

* * *

Anna held her head in her hands whilst Rob sat back in his chair.

"I'm so sorry, Anna, but it looks like it was your aunt's choice. In this new, crappy world, it's the best any of us are gonna get. She must have been such a strong woman," said Rob.

Anna's head whipped up. "Strong!" Shaking her head, she continued, "Surely the stronger thing to do is take your chances and stay with the people who love you?"

"No, Anna, you know she would never have made it out there. Maybe things were happening too fast and she did the only thing she could to help her son survive." Rob tilted Anna's face up to look at him. "Marcus would never have left her and probably have died in there too. Both of them horrifically."

Anna dropped her gaze back to the carpet, accepting everything Rob had said. The pain was unbearable as she rubbed at her chest; it was physical, and she needed it to go away. But at the same time, she wanted to feel every ounce of it, to fully mourn her aunt and the immense loss she was feeling now.

Her hand brushed against her locket, and she lifted it to her face, viewing its contents. Her mother smiled at her, looking so much like her aunt in their younger years. She shifted her gaze to the other photo, the one of her children, and longed for them. Then she thought back to her kind and wonderful Aunt Judy, missing her so much already.

"I can't even go see her," Anna said as tears began to flow. "And where the hell is Marcus? Did he even make it? What if he's out there now, looking for us?"

Rob stroked her back. "Look, I think we all should eat some food, then get a little rest whilst the dead are out there in full force. Who knows, they might hear something else and run off soon or gradually disperse. Either way, we shouldn't make a move with so many out there."

Anna nodded, looking downwards. She blinked a few times, noticing the tea towel wrapped around Rob's leg.

"What's that for? Has something happened? Are you ok?" Anna's heart began to pound. *It could be an injury from a zombie.* She hadn't even asked if there were any problems in her aunt's house. *So selfish, Anna.*

Jack came nearer, examining at his brother's leg. "You haven't been bitten or scratched, have you?" Jack's usual jovial nature had vanished; there was a slight quiver to his voice.

Rob waved his hands, palms forward. "No, no, no. Not at all, just calm down, both of you. Yes, I got into a fight with a zombie over at Judy's, but *no*, it wasn't the dead guy that did this to me. I landed on a plastic bin that ended up stabbing me..." Both Anna and Jack stared wide-eyed at him. "I promise, that's what happened."

Anna breathed out a sigh of relief, witnessing Jack relaxing too.

"Get your trousers off, Rob, I need to look at that wound," said Anna with a much more cheery disposition than she had intended.

"I can sort it out myself, honestly, don't worry about it," replied Rob.

Anna stared at him with her lips pursed. There was no way she was going to let him deal with it himself. "Don't be ridiculous. It's the back of your leg, I can do it just fine… Unless you're embarrassed, that is?" Anna teased. "And let's not forget whose hand happened to grab my arse earlier."

Rob's face dropped. "But… but I was helping you over the fence, away from the dead."

Jack guffawed. "Oh my God, did you?" His eyes and smile were wide with hilarity.

"Shut up, Jack," said Rob. "Anyway, I don't get embarrassed… If you want my pants off, then you can have 'em off."

Jack raised his eyebrows and said, "I'm gonna see what's in the kitchen."

"As quiet as you can please, Jack," replied Rob.

Anna watched Jack leave before saying to Rob, "Go on, then," holding back a huge grin.

Rob glanced over at Anna; she was eagerly awaiting seeing his strong legs. He twisted away from her as he unbuckled and pulled his trousers down to his knees.

Wow, that's quite an arse!

Don't be a perv, Anna. Fix the poor man's leg. She shook the dirty thoughts from her mind and got to work on Rob's injury.

170

* * *

Anna filled Jack and Rob in on what had happened with her family, right up until she literally ran across the two of them. Rob couldn't believe she'd ran at the zombies on purpose, then thought again: *of course, she would do that for her kids*.

Rob had chosen the armchair across from Anna to rest in. She was lying on the settee, facing away from the room. Although they had shared a few moments of banter earlier, he didn't want to leave her alone just yet. Jack had rustled them all up some food; there was still plenty in the cupboards here, so they wouldn't starve any time soon. The water and power were still working too, which was a good sign. *How much longer would they last, though?*

Jack headed up the stairs soon after he had devoured his crappy meal of junk food, looking for a decent bed to crawl into. He could still taste the cheese and onion crisps even though he'd finished with two mars bars. As he left, Rob reminded him to keep his boots on; if they needed to run fast, it could be the difference between life and death. Their packs and weapons were always left right next to where they were resting too. So many new things to consider in this uncertain time.

He watched Anna's back as she was curled into the sofa. He could make her out in the darkness pretty well and could see she was lying still, meaning no silent sobbing. She had perked up when looking after his leg but soon declined again, thinking about her aunt, Marcus, and whether her children were safe. He hated seeing her so distressed, but there was nothing he could do for her other than being there if she needed him.

Anna rolled over and faced Rob, speaking with a sleepy, husky voice that vibrated over his skin. "You're watching me?"

Rob did a little chuckle, caught out. "Not really, just making sure you're ok."

"Thanks," Anna replied. "But I'm not sure I am."

Rob gave her a weak smile. He so badly wanted to go to her and make everything feel good again, but now was not the time. He had been remembering how her fingers felt touching his skin and had to shove the thoughts away to concentrate on her emotional needs.

"I'm starting to believe none of us will survive this, so what's the point prolonging the inevitable? Maybe I should have taken some pills myself after giving them to my children. At least then, they wouldn't have to see the horrors out there."

Rob frowned and sat forwards. "Anna, don't say that."

"Well, it's true," she said before sighing and leaning back against the sofa.

Rob stood and joined her, sitting so that their knees touched. "Listen to me, Anna, don't you *ever* give up. If anyone can do this, it's *you*. You are an incredible woman, and I've witnessed you step up and do everything you had to do to save your children. The things I've seen you do and I've not even known you twenty-four hours yet… You're having a low moment, that's all." Rob took a few moments to steady his racing heart. "You can do this, Anna. And you will because you have to."

Anna smiled up at him and rested her hand on his leg. "Thank you… *so* much. You and Jack are a huge factor in me still being alive right now."

She kissed him on the cheek and stood, walking into the kitchen. He watched her walk away, still feeling her lips on his tingling skin. *I want her so much, but is it right?*

172

* * *

Anna poured herself a glass of water, needing just a minute to gather herself and wipe away her tears. She didn't want Rob seeing her in a state; she wanted to be the strong woman he said she was.

She felt him enter the room and was sure he was watching her again. She closed her eyes and remembered what it was like to kiss him, longed for it again. Hell, it might even cheer her up a little.

Anna twisted around to see she had been right; he was watching her, but with an intensity she hadn't seen since that first moment they had met. This was different, though. He was looking straight into her eyes instead of assessing her the way he had that first time.

She held his gaze and wanted to say so much but didn't know where to start. More than anything, she wanted him to close the distance between them right now. *Come on, Rob. I can't make the first move again and look like I'm desperate. Which I am, of course. A year without sex and even longer without regular sex. Shit, my last time was that guy I dated for two weeks before I gave up dating for good. Hell, just a snog and a bit of touching would be good.*

"Anna," Rob started but never said anything else. He looked like there were a thousand words on his tongue, but he couldn't get another one out. She could see his hands clenching a little whilst he looked into her eyes.

Rob inhaled and exhaled through his nose before striding over to her. Anna backed up to the worktop and placed her glass down. *I really hope he's going to kiss me now.* She looked back, and his face had stopped an inch in front of hers. He was looking down at her mouth. *Touch me, please.* She could smell his scent: leftover deodorant and a musky man kind of smell that made her crazy. She could feel the longing in him.

His left hand slid around her waist, and his right caressed her cheek, moving around to stroke her hair. His breath warmed her mouth when he lingered there. Their eyes met, and he finally brushed his lips over hers.

Anna kissed him back, softly at first, matching him. Then when his intensity increased, hers did too. He tasted of the orange squash they had all been drinking, and Anna loved how soft his lips were. His hard chest pressed up against her breasts, and she wondered what he looked like shirtless. He pulled her closer to him as she slipped both of her hands up underneath his t-shirt. She could feel every muscle rippling in his back.

His strong arms were wrapped around her, making every inch of her skin tingle with desire. She needed him right at this moment, not just to forget the crappy world outside but to make her feel like a woman. *I need to feel something other than fear right now. I wouldn't normally be so ready for it, especially after this short a time of knowing someone, but life could end the next time we step outside.*

Anna brought her hands around to the front and allowed her fingers to feel the soft hair on his chest. Rob moaned into her, then his hand slid down from her waist and cupped her arse cheek. *Oh my God, do I need this.*

Anna's hands found Rob's belt buckle and began to undo it. Rob breathed into her ear when he spoke, "Anna, are you sure?"

She looked him straight in the eyes and said, "Don't you dare stop."

Rob flashed a huge smile, showing all of his perfect teeth. "No problem."

* * *

Anna awoke on the settee, covered over with a blanket and little other clothing. She blinked away the sleep and could see that the dark room was empty. She dressed, struggling to find some of her clothing, and put her boots back on too. *Breaking all the rules here, not being ready to run.*

Anna found Rob in the front bedroom, evaluating the street through a crack in the lightweight, violet curtains. The colour matched the bedroom wallpaper behind the head of the bed. A delicate pattern of tiny purple flowers were scattered across the wall and when Anna looked around the rest of the room, she noticed the other small features that also matched. The slender vase with lilac coloured plastic flowers on the dressing table. The figurines on the chest of drawers and a narrow table runner over the top. And the few pieces of printed artwork scattered around the walls all had a hint of the same colour. *The lady of the house certainly liked lilac.*

Anna's attention drifted back over to Rob. He was standing with his arms folded over his chest, and she looked on in awe at his muscular body—something she knew pretty well now.

"How's it looking?" Anna whispered into his ear, taking up position next to him, feeling the warmth of his body.

Rob looked at her with a mischievous smile. "Pretty damn good from where I'm standing."

Anna laughed, feeling her face in full-on smile mode. "Out there, charmer… You know, where the *dead things* are walking around."

"Oh yeah, I'd forgotten all about them." Rob chuckled. "There's still quite a few out there, but I reckon at least half have wandered off elsewhere."

"Really?" Anna checked for herself.

"It'll be light again soon," said Rob. "I think if the back is clear enough, we could make a run for it. We're not that far from the countryside now; if we can leg it without being seen, then we should be a lot safer out there."

Anna nodded in agreement. "Oh, how does Jack know all of that geeky stuff he came out with earlier? And why do I get the feeling that was the tip of the iceberg?"

"Because it is, he's a bit of a clever clogs at his age. He was going to that Ron Dearing UTC, and he was absolutely flying there. Nothing like me at all," Rob answered, pride displayed across his face.

"Wow, he's a genius!"

"Yeah." Rob paused before speaking again. "Listen, I want you to have this."

Rob pulled out a flip knife and handed it to Anna. She screwed up her eyes, looking at the small knife, and wondered how much use it might be.

"I know it's a small knife, but that's what makes it perfect. Here…" Rob knelt in front of Anna and held her leg, "If you keep it on your boot like this, then should everything go wrong, you'll always have a backup." Rob stood, taking hold of Anna's hand. "I want you to be safe."

Anna's smile reached her eyes, then she leant forwards and kissed him gently on the lips. "Thank you."

"You're welcome."

"Well, I suppose we should go wake up Jack, get some food sorted, and make a move," suggested Anna.

"We should… but first I need to do something before Jack wakes up," replied Rob.

Anna was about to ask what when he kissed her heartily, pulling her down on the bed. She went along with Rob's plans more than willingly, allowing just a few more moments of happiness before they headed out into danger again.

Chapter 21

Anna readied her things in the living room whilst Jack and Rob did the same upstairs. She had gone through the downstairs cupboards to see if there was anything they could add to their supplies. There was plenty that she wanted but didn't want to carry, like the fully stocked alcohol cabinet and some hardback survival books. If she ever managed to return to loot for supplies, then she would surely come back to this house.

One thing she did take was several tubes of superglue. Marcus had cut the top of his head open once when Aunt Judy was away and didn't want to sit in A&E for hours; he asked Anna to glue the cut together. She hated the idea and would never have done it to her children, but Marcus was an adult, so she thought, *what the hell.* It worked a treat, so the superglue went in her bag.

Jack had his jacket on and backpack on his shoulders when Anna reached the foot of the stairs to see where the guys were. Jack was standing at the top, fiddling with his torch, when he managed to flick it on, illuminating Anna and the entire glass front door at the foot of the stairs. The whole thing lit up with Anna's silhouette framed there. *Oh, crap!*

Rob stepped out of the bedroom and immediately pulled the torch out of Jack's hands, pointing it at the floor instead. "What the hell, Jack? The dead are still—"

Pounding fists hit the door hard and fast, cracking the glass there in the first three seconds. Anna's head flung around in time to see the first hand shooting through the broken opening, closely followed by a head. She jumped back into the living room, slamming the flimsy door shut, pushed the armchair up against the door, then piled a small sideboard on top after hearing the dead's voices grow louder and start pounding the other side.

"Fuck. Fuck. Shit," she said at the same time the large living room window received its own set of thudding hands. "Why didn't I run up the stairs?"

Anna held her hands on top of her head, thinking. *They're gonna get in here in no time at all. Is this it?* She backed away from the window, thinking of Jasper and Alex. She touched the locket again, thinking of their smiling faces. They didn't bring tears to her eyes this time like they had so many times before; now the only thing she thought was *No, this isn't it. I will see them again... But how? What the hell do I do?*

Anna looked around the rooms, desperately searching for inspiration. Thudding feet from above rang out, revealing the infestation of the house. It sounded like there was a furniture removal company up there, too, with more dragging and banging sounds carrying down to her level. She glanced to the back doors, which were clear, then back into the room she was standing in.

I can't run without Jack and Rob; I need to slow them down to give us all a better chance. She clocked the brimming Alcohol cabinet. *That's it: the alcohol. I'll light the fuckers up.*

Anna snatched at the cabinet, pulling three bottles out and the matches she had retrieved from the kitchen drawer moments earlier. She opened the bottles and poured the contents over the sofa beneath the window and the armchair in front of the living room door. Memories of alcohol-fuelled nights flooded her brain as the vodka and whisky smells hit her nose.

Before she had the chance to light the furniture, the large window shattered, allowing greying arms to reach through the curtains. Faces and bodies of the dead were forcing their way through the massive window frame.

Anna struck the first match and sent it flying to the sofa, followed by a second and a third, then a fourth. The flames shot up at least three feet, already touching the dead that had managed to get most of the way in. Anna lunged forward and stabbed her crowbar through the first beast's face, then swung the metal at the head of a second.

The flames were rapidly rising now and had started lighting up the clothes of those who had clambered through. Anna went to head out of the back door, hoping that Rob and Jack were already jumping down from the upstairs window, but she halted mid-stride; more of the dead had gathered there, blocking off her exit. It hit her like a sledgehammer to the chest.

No, no, no, no, no, no. Anna nearly collapsed right there in that moment. *How can this be happening? It's not fair. I need to get to my kids!* Hopelessness washed over her, leaving behind only sadness instead of the fury she now needed. *I can't fight my way out of this; there are too many.*

The noises of the burning dead heightened behind her, and she wondered how many seconds she had left. The smell of burning furniture and flesh hit her hard too. Before she could sink to her knees, accepting her fate, plaster hit the floor next to her feet. More followed, hitting her head, drawing her attention to the ceiling. A hole appeared, and she could see the worried faces of Rob and Jack peering through.

Anna looked up in utter shock, her mouth wide open and unable to speak. Rob shouted, "Anna, fucking move. NOW!"

That was what she needed, an instruction to move, so that was what she did. New hope flooded her chest, making her jump onto the kitchen table just beneath the large hole in the ceiling. She pushed her rucksack up to Rob; at the same time, a flaming beast lunged towards her. *How can they be walking around whilst on fire?*

Anna unleashed a boot to the head of the monster, almost toppling herself from the unsteady table. Rob leant down through the hole, hanging his arms there for Anna to take hold of. She reached up as another flaming monster grabbed on to her legs.

Rob pulled at her arms but had the added weight and strength of the dead hanging off her feet. The dead man's burning arms began to burn Anna's legs, making her cry out in pain. Rob continued to pull her up with the dead guy still clinging on for dear life. Anna released one of her legs from its grip and stamped down on its head.

Rob yelled out, jerking Anna up the rest of the way through the hole. Jack took over, dragging her through, so she was now entirely in the bedroom at the back of the house. Rob rushed over to her and looked over every inch of her legs. They were burning, and while Anna hoped it was only superficial, she wondered if there would be any scratches there too.

"Nothing… I only see burns," said Rob with shaky laughter

following.

Anna released the breath she didn't know she'd been holding. "What now? You do know I've set fire to the house?" Anna grimaced, looking at the brothers' faces.

Rob nodded, smiling. "Yeah, I guessed that you had. The burning dead people running around down there gave it away."

"Cool. Nice one, Anna," said Jack, nodding his head at her.

Rob threw a dirty look at Jack before standing and storming over to the window. "Yep, the back way is fully blocked, too, and it's not going to take long for them to get in here, so… it's be eaten alive or burn to death?"

"Hmm, interesting choices," Jack joked.

"I'm sorry, guys," said Anna.

"You've done nothing wrong, Anna. You bought yourself those crucial few seconds that kept you alive," replied Rob.

Anna took in the room they were now trapped in; Jack and Rob had shoved the massive wardrobe in front of the door and had it backed up by a heavy-duty bed frame. *How long will it hold? Does it even matter if we're going to burn to death, anyway?*

"I've got it," said Rob. He looked at her and Jack with excitement in his eyes. "We use these bedsheets here to make a kind of rope. I'll jump from the window to the garage roof there, tie it off, and you two can shimmy down it across to me.

Anna and Jack joined him at the window. "Woah, are you mental? You can't make that jump. You're not spiderman," said Jack.

"I agree, that's a suicide jump. You will land smack bang in the middle of that growing crowd," said Anna.

"There's no time for any other solution. I'm doing it, end of," replied Rob. "Let's make a rope—unless you two want to jump as well."

Anna and Jack shared a horrified look. *Can he make that jump? Do we have any other choices?* Anna hated it but didn't know how to stop him; they had no other plan whatsoever.

"I hate this. You had better make it, or I'm going to kill you," said Anna.

Rob grinned back at her, then grabbed the bedding off the floor whilst Jack pulled some more out of the cupboard on the other side of the room. It took them just two minutes to fashion a makeshift rope. Smoke had started to billow out from the downstairs windows, and Anna was sure she could feel the heat through the floor. They had covered the hole in the floorboards using the mattress, hoping to block out the smoke and the deafening growls of the dead that gathered below.

Rob climbed out the window with the bedsheets tied around his waist and the other end attached to the bedframe at the door. He shimmied across the window to the farthest point, readying himself for the jump.

Both of his arms gripped onto the window frame behind his body whilst he faced the garage. He allowed himself to swing back, then used his strong legs to throw himself forwards, leaping through the air towards the roof of the garage like a flying squirrel. He reached out his arms when he neared the roof and hit the side of the wall hard, with a loud grunt. His arms held on to the rooftop, trying to grab onto anything that might help lever himself up; at the same time, the dead were trying to catch his flailing legs.

Jack had looked away when Rob had left the window, but Anna stared on, her hands gripping the window ledge like she could break the damn thing off. She leant forward, watching the beasts almost grabbing his feet, but he managed to pull himself up and on top of the roof.

Anna blew out a heavy breath, turning to look at Jack, who returned to the window. In that exact second, cracking sounds had them both turning their heads towards the bedroom door. It was starting to break now; surely, it wouldn't take the dead much longer to get through. The fire was getting closer, too, with darker smoke billowing in through their open window.

Rob had managed to secure the bedding to some kind of pole at the side of the garage, but it looked flimsy, so he took a firm grip of it too. Anna started coughing when she breathed in the smoke, pushing Jack up and onto the window ledge to go across to his brother. He began to cough, too, as he gripped the bedsheets. He levered his legs up over the makeshift rope and dangled, using his hands to shimmy himself along. It took only a minute for Jack to cross, so next, it was Anna's turn.

Anna climbed out the same way Jack had and grasped the bedding, shifting her grip several times. The smoke was getting thicker by the second, so she found it difficult to see what she was doing—the never-ending chorus of growls from below was also making the task much harder to concentrate on.

Anna tried to shuffle her legs along it the way Jack had, but struggled. She just wasn't confident at all, so her hands began to shake. Trying to calm her nerves, she blew out a slow breath, then inhaled the black smoke. She coughed again. *Just get on with it.*

She allowed the bedsheets to take her weight and dangled the same way Jack had. Her arms took the strain. It was already getting hard. Her fingers hurt like hell from gripping on so tight. She wasn't sure her tiny arm muscles could take much more of her own weight when loud cracks came from the bedroom she had just left. The growls grew more audible from below, sensing something about to happen.

The zombies smashed through into the bedroom, dislodging the bedframe, and sending Anna plummeting to the ground.

Chapter 22

Anna landed hard on two of the dead. They cushioned her landing in a way, but it felt wrong being on top of them whilst they squirmed. A waft of a bad smell had hit her when she landed too. The others were knocked back like dominoes, giving Anna a crucial couple of seconds to scrabble to her feet. She rolled off the dead and bounced straight up, shoulder barging the nearest zombie out of her way.

When she had knocked the dead down, it had created a temporary corridor to the next-door neighbour's fence. It had become a sort of death corridor, with grasping grey fingers and lunging bodies.

She righted herself after the shoulder barge and headed straight for the opening. Her right foot kicked out at a face that came within two inches of locking around her left leg. Another beast lunged at head height from her right, so she grabbed its clothing and swung it around, using its own momentum to push it away from her. *Come on, you bastards!* A third charged head-on directly in front, blocking her exit, so she used her boot to smash its right knee, sending it sprawling on the floor. It still tried to grab her as it went down, but Anna was too fast.

Within seconds, Anna had reached the five-foot fence that separated the two gardens and leapt at it, using her speed to propel her up and over with nothing resembling any grace. She was noisy and rough about it, but she got her arse over that fence and away from the dead that wanted her flesh.

"Go on, Anna," said Jack.

"Unbelievable!" Rob said.

Anna looked over to the roof of the garage, remembering they were there. She recollected some shouting when everything was happening but hadn't registered anything other than the dead trying to get her.

The fence Anna had just jumped over began to rock. The monsters hammered at it and pushed to get to their prey. *No rest for the wicked.* Anna shouted over to Rob and Jack, "I'm going to keep going through the gardens then meet you guys down the back alleyway. They should all follow me, anyway, giving you guys a way out."

Rob flashed Anna a thumbs up, then herded Jack away from the edge of the garage and the view of the dead.

Anna climbed the next fence using the internal cross panelling, hearing the first fence cracking and beginning to give way. She was already mounting the third one when the dead's growls grew in intensity and volume, crashing through the first.

Anna put four garden fences between herself and the beasts before they lost sight of her, allowing her to mount the foot of the garden she was in and enter the alleyway. Rob and Jack were already waiting there for her when her feet hit the pavement.

"That was incredibly close," said Rob, checking her over for bites again.

"I think Rob shit his pants when you fell into the zombie pit," Jack said, grinning cheekily.

"I think I shit my own pants, Jack," Anna replied. "It's a good job I've got clean underwear with me."

"I honestly thought I'd lost you then, Anna," said Rob.

"Yeah…" Jack bumped his brother on the shoulder. "I had to stop him from jumping straight down there with you."

"Well, no need. I had it covered. It turns out having a big arse is useful sometimes…" Anna muttered.

Rob grinned and stepped closer to her. "There's absolutely nothing wrong with that arse at all. In fact—"

"Ok, that's enough. I think we need to move," Jack interrupted.

"It seems as though you are embarrassing your brother," said Anna, smirking at Rob.

"Hmm, it does." Rob ruffled his brother's hair roughly; Jack swatted his hand away. "We *should* get moving, though."

* * *

The trio leapfrogged several gardens to head back to the main road once again. This brought them out much farther than they had previously been, and it felt like they were finally getting somewhere.

They travelled the length of Saltshouse road, not straying too far because of the Holderness drain coming up. The only sure way to cross it without diverting them too much was the Saltshouse road bridge. They travelled nearly one and a half miles before turning left onto Holderness road. This would, in time, lead them to the country roads they needed.

They hunkered down behind a group of hedges to scour the area around them once again. The length of the large main road stretched off away from them in both directions, but they only needed to make sure it was clear heading towards the country. The usually busy dual carriageway sat empty with its half-finished road works. Orange cones segmented the area to be tarmacked and made it look as if someone might return any time soon.

The plan was to continue along Holderness road, then Bilton village, all the way into the countryside, until Anna had a thought: "I've just realised there's a chemist on the other side of these houses. There's a row of shops, but I know there's a chemist too. I need to go and have a look; I'm sorry, I should have mentioned this before."

"Woah, why do you need a chemist?" asked Rob.

"Alex has epilepsy, and although we do have a small supply of medication for her, if I can get some more now, I have to."

Jack nodded resolutely. "We should try, Rob; it's important," he said.

Rob nodded. "Yeah, of course, it makes sense. I'm glad it's still dark too—gives us a slight advantage."

Anna was overwhelmed at how amazing these two people were. Their mother would have been so proud. "Thank you both so much," she said.

"Stop thanking us; there's no need now. We're a team," Jack said, beaming at her and Rob.

Anna and Rob both smiled, then Rob reached over and ruffled his brother's hair again; this time Jack seemed to allow it.

"Let's go do it then, whilst we have the advantage," Rob said.

* * *

The three of them crouched behind a set of bushes to view the chemist front and the other shops that lined this small street. Rob looked across to Anna and Jack. They both had their preferred weapons in hand: Anna's crowbar and Jack's hatchet.

Rob looked down to his own hatchet, listening for footsteps, shuffles, growls, or anything else that might suggest a nearby zombie. He edged around the hedge and viewed the street top to bottom, hoping the street light wasn't too illuminating for *them* to see *him*.

"All clear out there," Rob whispered whilst getting closer to Anna. "I'm just wondering where the back door might be, though. It's really open over there, and I'm guessing we'd have to break glass to get in too."

Anna pulled her lips to the side. "Mmm, you're right. There's gotta be a rear door, surely..."

"Don't call him Shirley," said Jack, stifling a giggle.

Rob looked at him deadpan. "You absolute fool."

"Oh God, that was bad," said Anna, smiling.

Rob exhaled, suppressing a chuckle. *How can my brother be a genius one minute and an idiot the next?*

"Come on, now's the time to move. Stay close," said Rob before crouch-running across the road and disappearing behind the side of the row of shops.

Anna and Jack followed, edging between the building and foliage. They were shielded from any unwanted eyes as they found the right rear door. Rob made light work of breaking into the chemist. *I should have done this in real life before it all went to hell. I'd have made a killing.*

They were in, but Rob realised there might be an alarm, so he shot into the building to find it.

"Rob… there's an alarm in this place and looks set to go off any second," said Anna.

It seemed Anna had found it first. Rob charged over to it, trying to understand what he was seeing, but Jack sauntered over and glanced at the white box on the wall.

"That's a silent alarm," he said plainly. "Won't pierce the night with noise, but the police will know about it… Are we concerned about the police anymore?"

Rob scratched the back of his head and shrugged. "Err… no, I guess not."

"You might be good at breaking and entering, big brother, but leave the techno side of things to me," said Jack with a smirk on his face.

"Hmm… what about random beatings and arse whoopings? I'm thinking I should be in charge of those," Rob replied, smirking back.

"Now, now boys…" Anna interceded. "Let's do what we need to and get out of here; petty insults can continue later." As she headed for the drawers of medication, she said, "Ooh, you guys should check out painkillers, anti-inflammatories, antibiotics, and anything else that might come in handy."

"Check out the looting lady over there," joked Jack.

Rob chuckled. "Yeah, but she's got a point. Before long, every chemist will be turned over; I'm surprised this is still untouched."

Jack strolled along the nearest shelf and picked up a random box of pills. "We'd better crack on, then."

Anna held up several small white boxes. "Wow, I'm shocked

there's this much here, considering my normal chemist was struggling. I think there are three months in here. Happy we checked this out, you guys." Anna flashed a relieved smile at Rob.

"In that case, so am I," replied Rob, grinning back at her.

Jack and Anna's backpacks were now stuffed full. His was too, so their job here was done. Anna said, "Well, I'd say we should get—"

"Shh!" Rob put a finger to his lips, eyes bulging.

Shadows moved beyond the window, creeping along and trying to stay hidden until the last moment. Three large forms arranged themselves spread equally across the large expanse of glass. The streetlamps behind gave them away though, stretching their dark shapes onto the pharmacy's shop floor.

"There are people outside. I mean actual people and not the dead by the looks of it," whispered Rob. Before he could say anything else, the large front window was smashed in, sending glass flying everywhere. A dark van pulled up outside, screeching its tyres when it braked.

Rob grabbed Jack and moved him quickly over to where Anna was standing. "We gotta go now."

But before they could take another step for the rear exit, the three men were entering the chemist through the now open window. Rob twisted towards them when they shone bright torch lights in their faces. Anna and Jack raised their hands to shield their eyes, automatically taking a few steps back.

"Who the hell are you?" said a deep and menacing voice.

Rob kept his eyes firmly on the three men standing in front of the broken window. He couldn't see if there were any more men outside but knew the excessive noise would draw trouble in just a minute or two. He assessed all three intruders from top to bottom through squinting eyes with the three torch beams concentrated on him. Rough-looking men, booted and holding weapons, two with beards and all three looking like they might be a problem.

"We're just leaving," Rob said, holding out his hands towards them. "Needed some meds for a child; now we're on our way."

Rob, barely blinking, allowed his body to relax so they wouldn't think him a threat. He was, of course, and as he eyed up the strangers, a plan formed in his mind about how to attack these people should it come to it. Only as a last resort, though.

The man who had spoken looked to the other two men before saying, "Ok, no problem with that."

He smiled a crocodile's smile—one that never reached his eyes. Rob had encountered many guys like this during his time in the Army. "Not to be trusted" was always the phrase that came to mind. The smiling man continued to speak, "We just want pain meds… You three seen anything like that?"

One of the other men panned their torch across to Jack, then Anna. The torch lingered on Anna, but he looked across at the third man. Rob couldn't see their expressions; they were standing too far back, but this situation was getting worse by the second.

"Yeah, there's plenty in those drawers over there. We'll leave you guys to it." Rob nodded and began to turn away, but not wholeheartedly, knowing their disapproval would come.

"I don't think we should let them go just yet," the tall skinny guy who had his torch trained on Anna spoke up.

Rob's skin prickled; the thing he feared the most was about to go down. He squared himself back towards the three men and allowed his mind to spin the plan through a few times.

The thicker-set man in front, who appeared to be their leader, narrowed his eyes whilst staring at Rob. "Really? You think we could take something else away with us?" he addressed his own people.

The tall, skinny guy took a few steps forwards, not taking his eyes from Anna, and allowed his torch to roam over her body. He licked his lips, making Rob's skin crawl and his anger bubble up. He was about to explode, and he'd take whoever was closest with him.

Chapter 23

He was just a few paces away from Rob now, off to his left a tad, which suited him just fine. Rob ran through the plan he had formed in his head:

First man slashed in the face with his hatchet. Second man would already be running at him, so a dip of the shoulder, and launch him overhead. Third man attacks, so he has to dodge before spinning and slicing up through his back. Second man almost back on him, where it's a one-on-one fight.

There were a few quiet moments whilst they all looked at each other, studying the opposition. The three guys kept glancing from Rob to Jack and Anna, then between themselves, silently trying to communicate with each other. Rob knew their kind of language, though; he'd known way too many men like these and could always predict their next moves. *I have to move first, take 'em by surprise.*

Rob darted towards the first and executed his plan. SLASH! Up through his chin and cheek, opening them wide and spurting blood everywhere. The guy didn't even see it coming with his eyes still glued to Anna, but before Rob could get to the second guy, an almighty roar of growls and yells from outside stopped the leading man in his tracks.

The main guy pivoted to see the other side of the broken window, then his comrade was dragged back through it, screaming.

Rob didn't waste a second before shoving Jack and Anna back through the entrance they had come. The screams of the man Rob had slashed through the face followed them as they fled. The three of them sprinted down the narrow corridor and out into the lightening world, dodging left. Rob, the last through the door, pulled it shut, hoping the dead hadn't mastered door handles yet.

"Stop," he said when they neared the bushes. "We shouldn't go that way; let's find a way through these bushes."

They crouched and scurried their way through, sustaining multiple scratches to their faces, and emerged on the other side. Anna was first out and was set upon by a beast straight away. Rob witnessed her bring her boot up into its chest, allowing a couple more seconds to attack it.

Jack exited second and joined Anna on the grassed area to the back of the shops. She jabbed the pointy end of the crowbar through the beast's eye socket, downing it easily.

"This way," Rob pointed to their right, which would lead them back the way they were initially headed.

They ran, all three of them full-on sprinting. Rob checked behind them a few times, checking for any followers, but nothing so far. The occasional zombie would throw themselves out in front of them, but whoever led the way would dispatch them in silence: hatchet to the head, crowbar pushed up through the jaw, hatchet swipe through the face.

They came to a roundabout which would lead them through Bilton. It was another estate but not as large. They desperately needed a stretch of countryside to get away from potential masses of the dead, but they had no choice. Just a little farther, and they would be hitting the country.

***

The three of them were glued to the main road once again. They jogged at a steady pace, keeping their eyes peeled for any movement. They would move one hundred metres or so down the road before ducking behind a garden wall or shrubs, then continue again should the coast be clear.

"I am so sick of the suburbs," said Jack, whilst they were hiding behind some wheelie bins at the foot of a garden.

"You and me both," replied Rob.

Jack sniffed. "These bins stink too."

"Have you smelled your feet lately?" Rob replied with a smirk on his face.

"I'm pretty certain I stink worse than that bin," said Anna. "All this running under stressful situations, and I'm rotting under this leather jacket."

"With any luck, we'll be able to get cleaned up soon enough," said Rob.

Anna blew out a slow breath, nodding at the thought of reaching Preston. Rob covered her hand with his; she looked up, and his mouth and eyes were smiling a knowing smile. She half-smiled back and squeezed his hand before scouring the streets again.

"All clear," said Anna.

They darted to the next safe spot, then the next, and the next after that. It wasn't long before Anna realised they were nearing a vast supermarket—one with a pharmacy. Anna eyed the building, wondering at the best way in and the chances of zombies being nearby or even inside. A high wall surrounded the loading bay, with barbed wire on top of it and tall metal gates. But the gates were wide open.

"I know what you're thinking," said Rob, assessing the large building in front of them.

"Even I know what she's thinking…" said Jack.

Rob exhaled before saying, "Do you absolutely have to go in there? Actually, don't answer that; it's a stupid question." He smiled at Anna.

"Look… I think I should do this on my own. It's not right you keep putting yourselves at risk for me, for *my* daughter. I'll run straight to the pharmacy, grab what they have for Alex, nothing more, and be straight back out," suggested Anna, chewing on her lip.

Rob shook his head. "Not a chance—"

Anna didn't let him say anymore: "I think it'll be better for you guys to guard my exit out here. If I get into trouble and need to run, I won't be able to deal with them out here too. I can outrun those things, but not if I'm blindsided once I come out."

Anna rubbed at the tension in her face, awaiting their answer. Rob looked to the floor, eyes darting around from spot to spot, considering Anna's idea.

"It's a good idea, Rob. I don't like her going in there alone, but we need to make her exit safe. It makes good sense," said Jack.

Anna's body relaxed at his answer, then Rob's eyes met hers. "I don't like it, but… it does make a crazy kind of sense." He looked back towards the vast building and continued, "Isn't the chemist in there towards the back of the building?"

"Yeah, it is. I was thinking of entering the loading bay just there; the gates are wide open," said Anna.

Rob nodded in reply, his brow scrunched up and jaw tense as hell. She could tell he *really* didn't like her doing this, but there was no talking her out of it. It was something she needed to do, and with Jack and Rob waiting for her outside, surely nothing could go wrong.

They reached the back of the supermarket where the gates had been left open and neared the loading bay. At least one of the large roller doors was up, exposing the warehouse part of the building.

"Wow, just think of all the food and bog rolls in there… If this shit continues, we should consider looting properly another day," said Jack.

Anna patted him on the shoulder. "One day at a time. The Army might sort this all out soon enough."

"You have more faith than I do," said Rob.

Anna looked across at Rob, studying his face. *Is there something he isn't telling us? If he only recently left the Army, he'd know something, wouldn't he?*

They reached the gates, where Anna left Rob and Jack on guard duty and ran to the building wall. She peeked around the corner of the roller door and took in the warehouse. There was a lot more daylight now, but the interior was still quite dark. Inside were row after row of boxes, all piled high on crates, with many shrink-wrapped, exposing what was inside.

Jack was right; if this thing was going to last, this was the place to come. *But then, wouldn't everyone else too?*

Anna listened out for any noises—from the dead or the living. If the last chemist was anything to go by, she needed to avoid living people too. Anna was a trusting soul at heart but knew this part of society and human nature would always be present, no matter what happened in the world. However, she would never turn her back on someone who needed help; it had been engrained in her from her parents, and Judy and Marcus too.

Anna looked back to the gates. Rob was stood bolt upright, eyes darting left and right before returning his gaze to Anna. She nodded to signal the coast looked clear and rounded the corner into the gloominess of the warehouse.

She tried to calm her breathing down, to stop the incessant noise in her ears. She needed to focus on what she was doing and needed to see and hear everything around her if she was going to get in and out safely. *With any luck, there'll be no one in here.* She gripped the crowbar and inched her way through the warehouse, heading in a general direction to where she knew the chemist to be.

She stopped suddenly, not sure if she had heard something or if it was her own heart pounding away. She dared not breathe, listening intently. The warehouse itself seemed to be making the odd creaking and groaning noises, but where did that end and *other* noises begin? She waited for a few beats more before moving along the box aisles again.

The warehouse was getting lighter as she neared the far wall. She emerged from the enormous rows she had travelled down and could see a door just a few metres away to her right. Anna stepped out, heading for the door and the supermarket beyond, passing another walkway.

Anna caught movement out of the corner of her right eye just in time to dodge a set of grey fingers reaching out towards her. Her hair moved and the air pushed past her as the dead hand reached out. She moved to the side, and the fingers grasped at her ponytail but didn't manage to grab on.

Anna spun whilst dodging, readying the crowbar. The beast wasted no time launching at Anna once again but not fast enough to outmanoeuvre her swing. The metal collided nicely with its head, which only managed to stun the creature. It threw itself at her once more, so she brought the crowbar around and embedded the hooked end through the bone.

The beast crumpled to the ground, taking the crowbar with it with a loud clatter. *Too fucking loud!* Anna regarded the dead creature with her weapon protruding from its head before bending to retrieve it. She yanked at it, but no movement.

"Shit, that's quite far in," she whispered to herself.

She pressed her boot to the creature's head and yanked again with more force this time. The crowbar was released from the skull of the dead thing, throwing Anna off balance and landing her heavily on her arse. She hit the deck with a spray of gore flinging from the creature's brain and the end of the crowbar, splattering Anna's chin and leather jacket.

"Ugh, this is disgusting…"

Anna wiped the potential virus from her chin using her sleeve and stood again, assessing her surroundings. She removed the gore from the crowbar on the dead thing's clothes. Everything remained quiet and movement free, so she proceeded to the open door and the much lighter supermarket.

The door was propped open by something, and when Anna looked closer, she realised it was a boot. She edged towards the door, viewing the supermarket through the gap, before poking her head through. The boot was attached to a leg and the body of a man—or what used to be a man, anyway. He was now torn to shreds, his whole torso opened up and pulled apart. It appeared that his head was caved in too. *Can these things continue without any internal organs?*

Anna had to shove the door open a little more to squeeze through but allowed the boot to continue holding it open if a swift escape became necessary. *Strangest doorstop I've ever seen. Although, it would've made a killing at Halloween.*

Anna figured out where she was in the supermarket relative to the location of the chemist. She had shopped here many times in what now seemed to be her previous life. She moved to her right but kept close to the wall, her eyes trained on the aisles she was passing.

Shelves still had plenty of stock on them, but there were signs of struggles up and down every walkway. Bodies were strewn everywhere, with pools of blood covering the polished floors. Stock littered the ground, too, many damaged but loads left there for the taking.

Anna crept behind the chemist counter, stepping over debris on the floor and moving around open drawers and fridge doors. People had already been in here and hopefully had already left. She wasn't there for pain meds or any other exciting stuff.

She moved to the drawers and searched for the correct alphabetical label, looking over her shoulder towards the rest of the store every few seconds. Bingo! She had found the label.

"Shit!"

It was empty of her daughter's meds. *It's ok, I'll find more chemists.* Anna screwed her eyes closed, not believing herself. *What if I can't?* She shook her head and swallowed, holding back the tears that threatened.

CLANG!

Anna's head whipped round to view the supermarket once again. She had allowed herself to get complacent whilst she wallowed in self-pity. *You still have to make it back to your children, so get the fuck out of here—NOW.*

Anna retraced her steps with her heart in her throat. She had killed a few beasts now, but every time she came up against one of those things could have been her last. Avoidance was key.

A woman's scream was followed by growls and heavy feet thumping around the shop floor. Anna ducked behind the fish counter when a flurry of noises filled the air. She couldn't see anything, but the noises sounded like they were getting closer.

She popped her head around the edge of the counter to see a woman running towards her, closely followed by three beasts. Anna's breathing skyrocketed not from fear but because of what she was about to do. *Avoidance... Yeah, right!*

She pushed to her feet and ran *towards* the chaos. She pushed her body forwards when internally she screamed *NO!* The woman yelled out when she saw Anna running in her direction.

"Help me, please. Help m—"

The woman crossed the supermarket's central intersection and was tackled from the side by another of the dead. The woman's eyes widened even farther, if it was possible, as she was dragged behind the end of the aisle and out of Anna's sightline. *It's too late.*

Anna skidded to a halt. One of the chasing dead things had followed the first live prey, but the other two continued sprinting for the second. Anna spun on the spot and retraced her steps, dodging to the right when she reached the end of the aisle. She placed her back to the shelves and readied her weapon.

CRUNCH!

She swung it with full force, connecting with the nose of the monster. It flew backwards into its pal, ending up in a heap on the floor. Anna wasted no time stabbing her crowbar through the beast's eye socket on top, pinning the second beast down with its weight.

A hand reached out from under the pile and locked on to her boot. She repeated the stabbing motion and stilled the second beast, then pushed the grey hand away using her other foot. She hated having to kill these things; for a start, they used to be human. Secondly, it was disgusting with the noises it made and the smells released when they died a second time.

More growls and disturbances rattled throughout the shop, so Anna stepped away from the dead beasts. She headed to the propped open door, making sure to shove the boot out of the way, closing it behind her.

She ran between the box towers to the roller door, letting the daylight guide her. As she exited, she locked eyes with Rob and Jack, still standing where she had left them. Anna allowed a smile to cross her face for just a second, loving the fresh air on her skin.

SCREECCHH!

Tyres on tarmac shredded Anna's moment of relief. A dark van was turning the corner of the supermarket road, heading straight for the gates and looking like it wasn't going to stop.

Chapter 24

A wave of relief washed over Rob as Anna dashed out of the warehouse but vanished when a van careened around the corner, headed right for them. He darted across to Jack's side of the gate, grabbing him by the sleeve.

"MOVE!" he yelled in Jack's ear, propelling him from his stationary position.

Anna moved to her left, headed in the same direction as Rob and Jack. There was a space that ran around the side of the superstore. Anna reached the side opening first and sprinted ahead, with Rob and Jack following close behind.

Rob looked over his shoulder, seeing that the gap was almost too narrow for the van but not narrow enough. It had to reverse to carefully enter the opening they were now running down. The sound of the reverse gear sung out as the pursuers pushed the van hard. Rob's eyes narrowed, wondering if this dark van was the same one from the chemist. *It's got to be; why else would it chase us?*

Rob faced forwards to see a fence up ahead. Anna clattered into the metal and squatted down, holding out her clasped hands for Jack to use. Rob chanced another look over his shoulder to see the van gaining on them. Fortunately, there was little space for the van's fuller speeds. That didn't stop it from scraping the walls, though.

Rob hit the fence next and used his hands to force Anna up on top of it. He then used all of his upper body strength to grapple his way to the top; the van screeched to a halt behind them. Rob dropped to the ground and rotated his head to face their pursuers.

Rob had been right; the very same thick-set man was staring at him as he climbed out of the van. He could see his features this time and feel the hatred oozing off the guy.

"Keep on running... you're gonna need to!" yelled the leader through the fence.

Rob joined Anna and Jack as they exited the enclosure onto the other side of the supermarket. This brought them out onto the massive car park. A look over his shoulder and he could see people running in and out of the superstore's main entrance. A tall guy in his thirties with dark brown hair and metal bar gripped in his large hands. An older woman in her sixties with greying hair hanging loose to her shoulders. And a group of three teenagers, two wearing beanies and the other with a red baseball cap on but all with hockey sticks. Some were using trolleys, others had armfuls of supplies. It wasn't long before screams joined the activity. Rob saw just one zombie... but that was all it took.

Anna pointed diagonally away from the building and said, "That way... It should take us across fields but straight to where we need to be."

Rob nodded and followed Anna and Jack, running across the supermarket car park, not looking back at the chaos unfolding at the store's doors.

* * *

They ran at full speed, crossing the empty overflow car park before climbing a small fence into a field next to the petrol station. A guy was pulling at the nozzles and pressing buttons at the unattended fuel station. Anna realised the payment machines had stopped the same way everything else had, meaning no pumping allowed. Fuel galore underground, but no way to get at it—conventionally, anyway. *That's the next thing people will be fighting over.*

"We'd better keep running; they might be driving round to catch us," said Rob, scanning the surrounding landscape.

They crossed a small section of rougher terrain before reaching a field full of crops. They weren't far off being harvested by the height of their growth. *Not going to be harvested this year.*

They weaved through the tall plants and pushed themselves hard, wanting to distance themselves from those people. Ten minutes later, Rob signalled for them to slow down a little. All three of them panted, resting their hands on their knees.

The sun had risen much higher than when Anna had entered the supermarket. Anna raised her face to the sunshine and allowed her skin to soak up the rays, controlling her breathing once again. The tall crops moved in the breeze, brushing up against them. *What's going to happen to everything now the world is falling apart?*

"What the hell is their problem?" asked Jack. "I mean, why're they so bent on chasing us?"

Jack didn't get it just yet, but he must in order to survive out here. Anna looked down, not wanting to say it out loud, and let Rob fill him in.

"For a smart lad, you missed what went on back there." Rob stroked the back of his brother's head roughly. "They wanted two things, whatever we already had in our packs... and Anna." Rob audibly swallowed.

Jack's eyes widened in shock; by the way his mouth opened and closed, it was clear he couldn't get his words out. He stood, looking from Anna, to Rob, then back again with his mouth gaping. Anna watched the poor boy shrink back in on himself, losing the cheeriness he usually carried around despite the living dead.

"It's ok, Jack, they didn't get anything from us. And we're not that far from safety now; it's through these fields and a small village." Anna attempted to smile, shoving the images away that her mind conjured up. The thoughts of what might have been had Rob not dealt with the men.

They continued through the fields in a South Easterly direction, walking instead of running but remaining vigilant of their surroundings. Silence engulfed the trio as they marched onwards, all three concentrating on their own feet hitting the dry dirt. Anna's were drenched in sweat; she dreaded to think what the smell would be should she remove her shoes.

Anna looked to Rob and Jack and decided she needed to break the melancholy mood. She wanted to get to know her comrades better, find out a bit more about them. It was strange how she could trust them with her life but knew nothing about them. "Guys, it's occurred to me that I know very little about you two, and you both don't know anything about me, other than I have two kids."

Rob cocked an eyebrow at her, then looked back at his brother before saying, "That's very true. Why don't you start,

Anna?"

She waved her hands. "Ugh, don't start with me. I'm boring."

"Go on, Anna, what do you do?" Jack asked, then amended it, "Or what *did* you do?"

Anna looked at the brilliant blue sky over top of the nearby trees lining the edge of the field. She chewed on her lip before saying, "It might not be over yet. But… I worked in a bank. Numbers are my thing, and oh my God, is it boring. I wish I'd done something else."

"Not too late to change. How old are you again?" Jack narrowed his eyes at Anna and suppressed a grin starting to form.

"Hey, you should never ask a lady her age," Anna frowned playfully.

Rob pointed at her. "Lady? I've seen you smash several zombies' heads in now. Anna… you're no lady."

Jack's grin spread wide across his face. "Ooh…"

Anna's jaw dropped in mock disgust, and she jabbed Rob in the arm.

"See, would a lady punch someone?" Rob said, barely able to contain his laughter.

Jack held his tummy, roaring with laughter. *Mission accomplished!*

A few moments passed before the laughter died down and Jack said, "We still don't know how old you are."

Anna narrowed her eyes at Jack but answered anyway, "Ok, I'm thirty-four. Yes, I know I'm old, Jack. No jokes, please."

Rob threw a cheeky smile at Anna. "You look pretty damn good to me for thirty-four."

Anna's couldn't hold back the smile that spread across her face. Jack groaned. "Oh my God, give it a rest, you two."

Rob and Anna both chuckled before Anna said, "Tell me about the Army."

Rob kicked at one of the larger mud heaps as he continued walking and waited a moment before replying, "Nothing to tell really… I joined when I was nineteen and got dishonourably discharged last month for attacking a senior officer."

"Woah… That's nothing to tell?" said Anna.

Jack jumped in: "The officer had it coming; he said some nasty things to Rob to rile him up. But it played into Rob's hands, because he wanted discharging so he could come back to me."

Rob glanced over at Jack, throwing a mucky look. Anna raised her eyebrows at the information but never for a second judged him.

"Ok… Well, I'm glad that guy got what was coming to him," said Anna, trying to catch Rob's eye.

He faced her, seeming a little stunned at her immediate acceptance. Anna reached out her hand and took hold of his, squeezing a little. He reciprocated and sighed, matching his pace with hers. They walked side by side across the field in silence once more—other than the odd joke that came out of Jack's mouth, anyway. Rob's hand was warm in hers, and everything about it felt right.

They travelled almost two miles and could see the road coming up just ahead. Rob suddenly stopped walking after he had been silent for a while.

"Listen, guys. Those fuckers in the van we came across, they might still be out looking for us. Not just that, but we could also come across others like them. People who want to take things from us, or just plain want to hurt us for the fun of it." Rob looked across at Anna, saying that last part. "I think we all need to be ready to do what needs doing if something awful happens."

"What do we need to do?" asked Jack eyebrows raised.

Anna looked across at Jack, hoping he would always be a little naïve. In this world they'd found themselves in, a lawless one, you might come across the worst of humanity. Anna really didn't like the thoughts that were being dredged up by this conversation. *Would she need to have this same chat with her kids about the boogeymen out here, seemingly around every corner?*

Anna faced Rob. "I'm not sure I could kill another human being, Rob. Even one that was trying to hurt me." Anna swallowed before continuing, "I… I'm not sure I could physically do it."

Rob walked over to Anna and held both her hands in his, saying, "But you might have to. If it's the difference between your life and theirs, you must. God, if it was your kids, I know you could." Rob looked pointedly at her now. "So… every time someone tries to take *you* away from your kids, don't hesitate. Guys like that, they're worse than the dead who want to feed on you. And after you, they'll find others to hurt."

They'll hurt others too… Anna stared Rob in the face, blinking several times before answering, "Well, let's hope it never comes to that." She remembered how easily Rob had dispatched the guy in the chemist. He had saved her, and she would be eternally grateful. But could she do the same? She touched her locket, wondering if she would have what it took in a dangerous situation.

They continued their journey across this particular field, the final one before the road that would lead to their destination. Anna kept her eyes focused on the uneven ground, careful not to twist her ankle on the earth's large ruts, but also still

211

pondering the darkness that had enveloped them all. Darkness that might continue should the horror not disappear. She looked up towards the sky, seeing dark clouds travelling overhead, concealing the sun. *How apt!*

"It's gonna rain," said Jack.

Anna hummed, surprised at how quickly the dense blackness had gathered up there.

"How far do you reckon now?" Rob asked.

"About fifteen minutes, we're literally around the corner."

* * *

They hit the road, and all groaned in unison. "That was tough," said Anna. "My legs are aching after that rough ground."

"At least it was dry," replied Rob, rubbing his thighs, remembering more challenging, wetter terrains. This was nothing compared to overseas, although he had never before had to kill the dead whilst fighting boggy landscapes. With a sigh, Rob looked up and down the road before saying, "Come on, let's keep going."

They plodded on down the centre of the road, with Rob checking over his shoulder every couple of minutes. He was sure those guys wouldn't let things go, but he hoped above all else that they wouldn't have a clue which way he, Jack, and Anna had gone, so had given up. They didn't seem too bright, but that main guy looked quite determined to inflict harm. Some people were just bent the wrong way.

As they entered the village, they all assumed caution mode once more. Although, so far, there didn't appear to be anyone around. They travelled down the narrow path that weaved around the church and past the butchers, heading for the traffic lights. Rob wasn't sure if he had been here before. Houses built long ago lined the road on either side. The church was the most prominent building, of course, with a short stone wall surrounding its grounds. Grass filled the space between the perimeter and the church building, with gravestones jutting up at regular intervals.

They rounded the bend where the church sat to view the traffic light intersection for the first time. They stood stock still, taking in the scene in front of them. There had been some kind of traffic pile up in this sleepy village; up to fifteen cars lined the street, some at odd angles and rammed into the vehicle in front.

"Mass exodus?" Jack asked.

"Maybe," Rob said, shrugging.

They moved around the first few cars seeing no one inside. There seemed to be supplies in each vehicle, like they had been headed somewhere else when this occurred. Most of the car doors had been left ajar, but some were still closed up tight.

Maybe the dead hadn't reached their streets yet and the people had had time to load their vehicles, Rob thought. *Didn't help them, though, did it?*

They moved towards a Land Rover Discovery, with Jack out in the lead. He edged his way past a tight spot with his face pressed up close to the vehicle's glass. A zombie struck the window from inside the car, hitting it with its fists and snarling at its intended victim. Jack threw himself away from the threat, almost smashing into the windscreen of the Ford Focus next to it.

He panted and held on to his chest before realising he was in no immediate danger. The beast continued to thud the glass with both hands, growling at them all, its mouth opening and closing as if it could bite them through it.

Rob took a closer look into the car, seeing another dead body seated next to the growling one. It had a screwdriver pierced through its eye socket and looked around fourteen or fifteen years old, judging by its size and clothing. He was just a kid like Jack but was now sat with a screwdriver sticking out of his face. Rob walked away from the vehicle and grabbed his brother's hand, helping him climb down off the bonnet.

They traversed the rest of the vehicles and came to the traffic lights, where they turned left.

"It's just up here, guys, past a few bungalows and smaller houses, then onto their grounds on the right-hand side." Anna beamed as she said this. Rob couldn't be happier for her to be reunited with her children. He prayed to God they were there.

But he frowned; something seemed out of place.

"What's up?" Jack asked.

"Can you hear something?" said Rob.

They all listened as the sound became known to them.

Chapter 25

Anna squinted, trying to make out the car approaching them.

"It's a small van of some kind, a white one," said Jack.

"Not those guys, then," said Anna, relaxing a little.

Rob hummed. "Could still be dodgy people, though…"

"Could be people who need help," replied Anna. She needed to believe there were plenty of good people in this world. People like them who would help where they could.

"I think we need to get out of the way here, just in case," said Rob.

"Don't be so suspicious, Rob. It's more than likely that they'll just drive on past, anyway." Anna turned away from the vehicle getting closer by the second and pulled Jack with her to the side of the road. Rob lingered behind. The rev of the van's engine increased in volume as it neared, making Anna turn to view it once again. She frowned when the van revved even louder, suddenly speeding up.

Rob became the van's target. She screamed out but had no clue what she said as the event was happening in slow motion. Rob tried to jump out of the way, but it was too late; it struck him, sending him flying into a nearby ditch.

A jolt of fear shot through her entire body, paralysing her. She was rooted to the spot when she lost sight of Rob and two men dived out of the vehicle that had hit him. Jack sprinted past her towards his brother, yelling something that Anna couldn't comprehend. Then a flurry of activity happened before Anna's eyes as the world spun around her head.

Anna's feet started to move and life came into focus again. "Nooo!" she shrieked as one of the men attacked Jack. He took a hit across the face and crumpled to the ground. Incapacitating panic flooded Anna's system and crept up her body. She managed a few more stuttering steps towards Jack before the guy from the chemist filled her vision. He stepped in front of her, blocking her way, and she halted to not bump into him.

Anna's head jolted backwards to pull as far away from this man as possible. *How? How? How?* She wanted to turn and run, but her feet were glued to the spot once more.

The man leant down and pulled the crowbar from Anna's hand. Her gaze snapped down to the weapon that had been taken from her. *SHIT! Wake up, Anna.*

Anna's breaths came in and out in rapid bursts whilst the man leered, looking her up and down. She craned her head to try to see Jack, but he moved to block her line of sight again. He smirked at her, nearing her face and breathing on her. Anna turned her face away at the smell, repulsed.

"Look at me," the man whispered close to her ear.

Anna never moved; instead, she stared at the ground, wishing it all away. Wishing Rob and Jack were ok and these men would just leave. Wishing someone would turn up and help them the way they would help others. Wishing the dead hadn't risen, and they weren't faced with this right now.

"Look at me!" he shouted this time and, grabbing her chin, forced her face around.

Anna closed her eyes to block out his disgusting face and any thoughts of what might happen next. He unleashed a backhand across her cheek, throwing her to the ground, then dragged her up again.

Her nostrils flared, and she swallowed down the bile rising from her stomach. *Rob! Jack!* They had possibly killed her friends and were about to take what they wanted from her. The other guy reached them, moving around behind her, and tears rolled down her cheeks.

Her backpack was pulled from her shoulders and placed on the ground next to her. The quiet scrape of zip ties being used entered her consciousness, and her hands were pulled behind her back, the ties closing around her wrists. She tugged at the restraints as claustrophobia threatened to overtake her. Then they shoved her forwards to the small white van, making her stumble.

They walked her past where Jack had been attacked, and she stared at his lifeless body, willing him to move, to be ok. The familiar panic rose; it was something she thought she had left in her past. It tickled the backs of her eyes, her vision blurring and her body tensing with dread and regret. The leader man walked past Jack, throwing a vicious kick into his abdomen. Anna flinched and cried out at the sight of it.

She tried to see Rob, but he was too far into the ditch. *Oh, God, please be ok. Please don't be dead. Please let this all stop now. Please, please, please.*

217

* * *

SLAM! SLAM!

Car doors slammed from far away. His head buzzed, and his face hurt so much more than it ever had before. *A car?* Tyres were rolling by on the tarmac near to him. *Where am I?* A car engine accelerated, moving up through the gears and then getting quiet again.

Jack's eyes flew open. *Rob! Anna!... Oh, shit, the car isn't a car; it's a van.* Jack surveyed the area from the ground, noticing the white van was gone. He tilted his head back to view the road, only to see the van disappearing into the distance.

He swung his head around in all directions. Pain speared through his nose and skull, so he closed his eyes against it. He touched his nose, feeling blood oozing from it. He could taste metal at the back of his throat and wanted to be sick. *Ugh, why does this hurt so much?*

"Anna," said Jack, far quieter than he had intended. "ANNA!"

Jack managed to roll himself up into a sitting position, grunting with pain and holding his stomach and ribs. He looked around again before forcing himself off the floor. He stood on unsteady feet and needed a moment of resting his hands on his knees before he could move again.

"ROB!" He stumbled towards the ditch, dreading what he might see there. "Rob, can you hear me?"

Jack tried to stand to his full height to view the ditch better but couldn't manage it. He clutched his left side with his arm and inched closer to where his brother had been thrown. Finally, he reached a spot where he could see the body of his brother. His lip quivered.

* * *

Anna had been thrown into the back of the dingy white van, while her backpack and crowbar were taken to the front with the men. The van had wooden panelling throughout with paint splodges and oil stains. A few discarded rags and a bit of rubbish lay in the far corner and the stench of stale water hung in the air adding to the already dismal environment.

She lay on her side, crying without sound at the thought of Jack and Rob. She hadn't seen Rob when she was bundled into the back of the van, but she had seen him hit with it. He had flown through the air like a rag doll. Metal hitting muscle and bone had Anna cringing and gagging at the thought. *Could he have survived without too much damage?* Even if he was alive, any broken bones would leave him vulnerable to the dead lurking nearby.

Poor Jack had been beaten up; he was just a kid. He didn't deserve this, and neither did Rob. All they had done was help her get to her children. She was so close, too; Jasper and Alex might have been inside their grandparents' house when she sped past in the van.

Anna stared at her locket lying on the floor in front of her. It was still attached around her neck, and she longed for the feel of the metal on her fingers. For some reason, the silver locket brought a sense of calmness to her, or at least made her feel closer to the people inside it. She couldn't even touch it right now with her hands restrained behind her back.

It's all my fault; I wouldn't listen when Rob tried to tell me. I've got him and his brother hurt, or even worse, killed. I'm such an idiot, and now I'll never see my kids again. I deserve this, to have these bad things done to me, whatever they will be. It's all my fault.

Anna to bounced around as they travelled down the road. She felt pain every time she hit the hard, metal floor after a big bump, but she liked it. The pain helped bring her out of the panic; it was a real feeling and not a made up one inside her brain. But she had also earned the pain; it was hers to feel, and she deserved it one-hundredfold.

She curled up as best she could with her hands tied behind her back, bringing her knees up close to her chest, and continued to sob. *Go on, cry like a baby. That's all you're good for, anyway.*

Her misery continued to envelop her, but not for much longer. *After all we've been through, for it all to go to absolute shit in a second... What the fuck! I learnt how to kill flesh-eating zombies just to get to my kids. I forced myself out of my house and ran from the dead to get to my kids.*

Anna sniffed up, feeling the tears subside and anger beginning to build.

Why, God, did you let me get through all of that to take it all away again? Ha, does God even exist when horror like the living dead are walking the streets?

Anna blinked away the remainder of the tears and looked around the van's interior, but it was empty. She looked down at herself, seeing the grime and flecks of blood splattered up and down her clothing. *I did that. I splattered the blood of the monsters. I killed them.* Her boots had seen her run so many miles when being chased by those creatures. *Even when I couldn't kill them, I could run.*

Anna blinked before widening in her eyes as she looked down at her boots. She had a knife wedged down the side of her right shoe. Rob had put it there so she could protect herself should any bad situations occur.

Well, what the fuck is this?

Anna shook away the thoughts that had begun in her mind. She couldn't fight two grown men, both vicious and all too willing to kill. There was no way she could do anything like that at all. She had barely survived out there as it was. If it hadn't been for Jack and Rob, she would have been ripped to shreds by now, never to see her children again.

My children! My Alex and Jasper are probably right back there at their grandparents' house.

Anna looked towards where the two men were sitting, feeling fury build within her. Those bastards had taken her away from her children. They had possibly killed Jack and Rob too. But what could she do about it?

Wimpy and scared Anna, you couldn't fight them... Or could you?

* * *

Jack crawled into the ditch next to his brother. He was lying face up, with blood streaked down his face. His arm was bent at an awkward angle, and Jack cringed as he tried to rouse him. If he could be awakened, anyway. The grassy bank behind Rob held some of his blood. Mostly sun scorched earth and foliage lay either side of him with just a few hints of green poking out here and there. The sun had been brutal on the greenery so far this summer.

"Rob… Rob, can you hear me?"

Jack leant towards his brother's face the best he could, given

221

he had a few broken ribs himself. He held his face close to Rob's, attempting to feel for any breaths coming out of his mouth. Simultaneously, he checked for a pulse in his neck, praying he would feel one.

Jack waited for what felt like a lifetime, shifting his fingers around and wondering if he had the right spot. He had always found it in the first aid lessons.

Dudum, dudum, dudum...

"Yes, you're alive. Rob, can you speak? Can you hear me? Wake up, Rob, you've gotta wake up," Jack pleaded with his brother whilst trying to keep his tears under control. "Please, Rob. I can't lose you too, not as well as Mum. Please."

A groan emanated deep with Rob. Jack wasn't even sure it came out of his throat.

"Rob, Rob, are you ok? Can you hear me?"

"Jack…" Rob breathed.

"Yeah, Rob. I'm here; what is it?" Jack replied.

"Stop shouting in my earhole, mate. You're killing me," said Rob, face pulled into a tight grimace.

Jack laughed and cried at the same time. He was a complete mess and didn't care that his big brother could see him doing it too. The relief of Rob being awake and alive washed over Jack; he never knew he could feel so many things all in one go. The pain washed over him next, making him remember it all. The car hitting his brother, then the guy smashing him in the face. *Bastards. He wanted to kill them himself. Never before had he wanted to hurt someone else.*

Jack sighed before saying, "Right, what do we do now, Rob?"

Rob shifted around, grimacing. "I don't know, Jack, I'm pretty messed up here. I'm sure I can't go anywhere right now."

Jack mentally catalogued Rob's injuries and knew he was right. And they were just the ones he could see. Rob's leg looked kind of iffy, so there was no chance of them walking away from here.

"Anna? Where is she?" Rob asked between groans of pain and shifting around to find a more comfortable position.

Jack looked away from his brother in the direction the van had travelled, then gazed down at his shoes as he squatted next to Rob.

Rob lay his head back against the mud bank behind him, understanding. "The fucking van," he said quietly.

Jack looked watched his brother's eyes and noticed, for the second time in their lives, tears forming there.

Chapter 26

Poor Anna. Jack realised what men like that would want with a woman. They hadn't wanted to take anything from them, just Anna, like Rob, had warned them about. *I've gotta grow up now and stop being so stupid.*

He looked up to view the road and their surroundings in general. He was trying to form a plan to get his brother out of this ditch and to safety. If any of the dead came around now, they could be done for.

He looked back towards the traffic lights, thinking of the cars there and if any looked like he could get it out of that mess, then looked back in the direction the van had travelled with Anna in the back of it. His mind faltered and despair began to claw at him. *Gotta think of something, Jack.*

That was when he noticed the driveway that intersected large trees and bushes on the other side of the road. His eyes narrowed, trying to see what was there better. *Is that where Anna was taking us?*

"Stay here a minute, I'm just going to check something out," said Jack.

"Is that supposed to be a joke? Where am I gonna go?"

Jack chuckled when it shouldn't be that funny. The gravity

of the situation lifted a tad, and his face relaxed from smiling. It hurt like hell to do it, but he couldn't help it.

He scrambled out of the ditch, holding on to his side. *Oh shit, that hurts.* He stood on the roadside for a moment and breathed in the air, hoping the nausea would bugger off. A few more deep breaths in, and he straightened as much as he could before walking towards where he thought Anna had been leading them.

As he neared it, he could see a large wooden gate on tracks and a fence stretching out from it in both directions. A car was parked there and couldn't be seen from down the road. The area was shrouded in foliage, with giant trees stretching up into the sky beyond the fence. *This has got to be it; it looks just like Anna described. Now, how do I get in?*

Surveying the gate, he realised it must be electric and needed a code to get in. He looked around and saw a small box on the side with what looked like numbers from this far away. He took a closer look and cursed. *Shit! It looks broken.* Jack grimaced, touching his side. He chewed on his bottom lip and looked about again for something to help him. *The car!* He walked over to the driver's side and shimmied himself in. *Shit, that hurts! Man up, Jack, Rob's in worse pain right now... he needs you.*

There was a slight decline in the driveway leading to the gate, so Jack released the handbrake and pushed the ground with his right foot. It inched towards the entrance, making Jack grin from ear to ear. *Shit, my nose hurts when I smile.*

So stop smiling like an idiot, then.

He pulled the handbrake back on, getting close to the gate. Eased himself from the driver's seat and headed around to the front of the car. With his long legs, he stepped onto the bonnet with ease and moved closer to the gate.

Peering over the top, he could see that the driveway snaked through dense trees and bushes and rounded to the right approximately one hundred metres down. A large, older looking house loomed over the top of some of the trees, with the attic windows in sight. *Woah.*

The sky had grown much darker in the last few moments, and spots of rain began to hit the ground and Jack's head. He looked up to the sky momentarily, wishing for just a little longer to work his plan through, then eased himself down from the car and did a fast walk back to Rob.

* * *

Rain started to patter on the roof of the van, and Anna could hear the swishing of the windscreen wipers. It had been coming for a while now; the dark clouds had gathered more prominently as the van's interior matched the outside world and darkened even further.

Anna tried to push the darkness within her away but struggled. She had always suffered from dark thoughts, but over the years had learnt how to bring the light to the forefront. This kind of situation was unquestionably the worst she had ever experienced, so if she found it harder, could she blame herself? Even so, a plan began to form in her head of how she could take these two guys out, but fear and uncertainty crept in.

What if I can't?

Then they'll still kill you, or worse, keep you alive as their toy.

Anna shook away the thoughts, not wanting to let them go any further. She closed her eyes tight, willing the voices that taunted her to leave and not hold her back. They had held her back her entire life. Fear, panic, and anxiety were all her usual companions.

Her children's faces drifted through her mind; images from when they were babies, toddlers, then growing up to what they were now. There is still so much more to see. *I don't want to miss out on the rest.* She realised she was holding firm in her hope that they had made it to their grandparents'. *Why the hell wouldn't I?*

When it came to her kids, that's when her strength shone through. That's how she had managed to get as far as she had through the hellhole streets she called home. Rob's words rang through her ears now: *"God, if it was your kids, I know you could."* He seemed to know her well already.

She thought back to being out on the streets with her children and Steve. She killed a zombie that attacked Steve, and his words came to her too: *"Who the hell are you now?"*

She had changed so much already; she'd learnt to deal with the dead when so many people couldn't. She mentally totted up the events of crossing some of Hull's estates. She'd got to her children, then led the dead away to help them escape. She'd saved Jack's life too. *Why the hell can't I do this?*

"You can do this, Anna." Rob had believed in her even when she hadn't believed in herself. If anything, he and Jack deserved her fury. They deserved her fighting the motherfuckers that had hurt them. They deserved retribution.

Anna's breaths were coming in and out faster now, and her nostrils flared at the increased volume. Her eyes were wide open, staring at her boot. They were wide open to what she had to do too. She could and would kill the fuckers driving this van. She just had to get a move on before they arrived to wherever they were taking her.

* * *

"Rob, I think I found Anna's ex-in-laws' place. I'm gonna go in." Jack looked down at his brother in the ditch with excitement. Rob's eyes were closed, though, spreading panic through Jack.

But Rob pried open his eyes. "Go careful, little brother."

Rob shivered, and his eyes fluttered closed once more. Jack scampered down into the ditch using his good side, removing his jacket and covering his brother up. He could see they might have more severe consequences if he didn't get help.

Climbing back out of the ditch was now more difficult with the rain coming down quicker, making the banks much slicker. He managed to crawl out and moved back to the car in front of the gate. Climbing back onto the bonnet of the vehicle, he studied the gate for the best way over. No matter what, it was going to be an effort with broken ribs, but he would just have to power through. His brother needed help, and fast.

Jack reached up for the top of the gate, feeling the pull to his left side, and bit back the pain that stabbed him there. He found a foothold to the side of the gate on the bricked-up columns holding it all together.

You'll only get one go at this, so make it the best you've got. Jack took a deep breath in; he pushed his foot against the brick column with all of his might, using his right hand to pull himself up and his left for balance.

"Aargh!" Jack screamed out in agony but never stopped pushing and pulling until he was on top of the fence.

He sat there, balanced precariously, but not being able to move just yet. His ragged breaths came in and out, with his heart pounding in his chest. His left arm was pulled in close, allowing only a moment's respite until he had to move again.

It's a good job I love you, brother. Jack opened his eyes again when the awful pain had begun to recede just enough to feel human. He focused on the ground on the other side of the fence and geared himself up to drop down.

Jack swallowed before counting himself down. *Three, two, one.* He let himself drop, and his feet hit the tarmac. The thud shot up through his body and out of his ribs. He leant over to the side and vomited, with agony piercing his ribcage. *Throwing up is not helping the pain.*

Jack quivered, trying to right himself, and wiped the sides of his mouth. He closed his eyes, thinking of his brother once more and the bastards who had hurt him. Rage bubbled up and propelled him towards the house.

The pain became more manageable as he neared the end of the long driveway. The trees that towered above sheltered him from the rain that was coming down heavier. *Get a move on, Jack; Rob's getting soaked and colder by the second.*

Jack had read many books on survival from the likes of Bear Grylls and Ray Mears and knew of the possibility of shock setting in. He had to help his brother.

The large front door appeared from around a wall of foliage. It had ornamental brickwork in the shape of a pointed archway and a covered porch area. The door itself was a huge wooden thing with massive metal hinges stretching across.

Jack climbed the three stone steps that had decades' worth

of grooves in the centre and knocked at the door. *Please be there, Steve. Please.* Jack jiggled up and down on the spot whilst still holding on to his ribs. The adrenaline was just too much for him to bear.

He leant into the door, listening for any signs of movement on the other side. The rain was hammering down harder now and made it impossible to hear anything in the house. *House? More like mansion.*

Jack realised *he* probably wouldn't open this door to anyone under these circumstances, so he decided on another approach.

"STEVE! IS STEVE HERE? I'M A FRIEND OF ANNA'S!" Jack yelled through the door as loud as possible in case they weren't just on the other side of it. If there was anyone in there, anyway.

"STEVE!"

Clunk.

The door had been unlocked and was being opened—*thank God*—only for it to be replaced by the barrel of a shotgun.

Chapter 27

J ack flinched backwards and nearly fell down the three stone steps. He righted his position and held his good hand out in front of him, towards the gun and the man holding it. *An actual gun!*

"Woah, dude. I… I… I'm here for help… St-Steve? Is Steve here?"

"Who are you?" said the man, staring down the barrel of the gun at Jack. He was an older guy with grey hair; old fingers curled around the shotgun. But he looked like he had used one before—*definitely something to fear.*

"I… My name is Jack, and I'm a friend of Anna's. We… me and my brother have been helping Anna get to her kids and Steve. And then we found her running from loads of zombies *again...* And we've travelled here with her to get to her kids… Jasper and Alex?"

Jack was babbling and couldn't help any of it but continued, anyway. The old guy's glare relaxed a little, and he raised his head from the sight of the shotgun, lowering it a tad.

"Where is Anna, then? If you're telling the truth, why isn't she here right now?" the old man demanded.

Jack sighed and dropped his hands. "Because she was taken."

* * *

Anna shuffled her body so that her hands were farther down, just past her bum. She wiggled and moved around some more until she had managed to push both her hands underneath. She rolled herself, so she was sitting upright with the tie wraps below her knees. They had looped several of them through each other, giving her more room to manoeuvre. *Idiots.*

Next, she had to slip her booted feet through the makeshift cuffs, bringing her hands to the front. She squirmed, trying to get the right angle and finding it difficult with such clunky boots, but eventually succeeded. It brought back memories of Alex trying to get her Doc Martins through the gap in the car's front seats to get in next to Anna. *My girl!*

Bringing her mind back to the task in hand, she reached forwards and retrieved the flip knife from inside of her right boot. Anna flicked it open, studying the small blade she would use to kill the two men. *I CAN DO IT; I WILL DO IT.* She allowed the words to roam through her mind like a mantra, egging her on and making her believe.

Anna's plan had banked on her keeping her tie wraps on her wrists. She would surprise attack the first guy with the knife but wouldn't have the same advantage over the second man. The tie wraps would allow her to compensate for her lesser strength. *Good planning might be able to overcome brute force—if it works.*

The sky had blackened considerably, meaning that the back of the van was shrouded in darkness. Another point for her attack. She pushed herself up onto the balls of her feet and crouch walked closer to the back of the men's seats whilst the van rocked from side to side.

Anna was on the passenger's side of the vehicle and had already decided that he needed to be neutralised first. The driver still had to drive, right? She inched forwards, eyeing the driver, hoping he wouldn't turn at the wrong moment or see her out of the corner of his eye.

This is it, Anna. Get it done and get it done right.

Anna held out the small knife in her right hand but steadied it with her left, preparing for what she had to do next. She narrowed her eyes, focused on the guy who had struck Jack in the face. She was about to make him pay.

In a flash, Anna pushed her body up and forwards to the right of the passenger. She had brought the knife level with his throat and then drove in at a downward angle, deep into his neck, feeling her fist thud against his collar bone. She pulled the knife free and struck again and again, stabbing him multiple times, feeling the sticky wetness coating her hands. *Nothing. She felt nothing.*

The driver, the leader, started shouting at her as he attempted to keep the van under control. His left hand darted out towards Anna's, but she pulled it away too fast for him, slashing the knife through the air. It was awkward with her left attached to it, but she managed ok.

He lashed out again and grabbed on to her with a strong grip. Anna switched the knife from her right to her left hand and stabbed him in the arm. He screamed out but didn't release her. *He's a strong fucker.* She drove the knife towards his face this time but was blocked. Her left hand was not as strong and controlled as her right, and it was still attached to the other.

The blood that coated the knife made it hard to keep hold of, therefore slipping away from her. She used her left palm instead to ram the guy's nose up into his face. Those half a dozen self-defence classes had resurfaced. She connected well but still didn't have the strength to stop him. He grunted but nothing more.

Anna concentrated on freeing her right arm, which would also give her left more freedom. She twisted with all of her strength, rolling her arm away from him and freeing herself, but flew across the van, hitting the wall.

Anna never paused; she lunged at him again with both hands outstretched and lifted them straight over his head, each arm on either side of the headrest. The man hadn't seen her coming from behind and ultimately didn't react fast enough.

Anna pulled her whole body backwards, allowing her restraints to now become the man's strangulation device. The tie wraps were pulled tight against his throat before he could get his hand up in the way. He could only tug at the tightening black plastic that was cutting off his airflow.

Anna leant into the back of the van, pulling with everything she had; the van started veering wildly across the road. She raised her right foot off the floor and pressed it against the back of the driver's seat whilst her wrists pulled at the restraints. Her hands were either side of his face and beginning to shake with the sheer force of pulling.

The plastic dug into her wrists, cutting her open and had her crying out in pain. She wasn't going to release him, though, not a chance, not until that bastard had stopped breathing and run them all off the road.

Gargled noises carried through to her ears, and she could feel both of his hands clawing at hers. The van swerved violently to the left, following the camber of the road. Anna felt the moment they left the safety of the tarmac and hit the grassed verge, bracing herself for the crash that was to come.

* * *

"I'm Steve."

Jack swung round to see him and breathed a sigh of relief.

"What do you mean she was taken?" Steve asked.

"A van with two men ran my brother over, attacked me and took her with them. I came to just as they were driving away. I'm so sorry, Steve." Jack shook his head with sadness, then said, "The kids, Alex, Jasper, and Logan? Did they make it ok too?"

Steve rubbed his hand over his stubble, then said, "Yeah, they're all fine, thanks to Anna. And I guess you and your brother too." Steve nodded towards Jack with a grateful smile. "Where's your brother?"

"That's why I'm here. I need your help," said Jack.

* * *

Anna's eyes opened, and she mentally felt around her body. She was lying in the back of the van still, but she was sure it wasn't the floor that she was on now. Rain continued to hammer on the van's metal as she tried to focus her eyes on the dark interior.

She turned her head to the side, seeing the backs of both seats in the front of the vehicle. She had been propelled forwards, hitting the back of the driver's seat, then flung to the left when the car rolled. The seats jutted out from the right as if coming from the wall. Both men had been wearing their seatbelts and were still strapped in, with the driver hanging from his.

Anna had flown around the interior of the rear compartment like a lone trainer in a washing machine. Her head, ankle, and back hurt, but other than that, it was mainly her bleeding wrists that were causing the most pain.

She crawled to the front of the van, where neither man was moving. She hadn't expected the guy she had stabbed in the throat to still be alive, but she had seen enough movies to know that bad guys always came back somehow.

She moved to the front section, seeing the leader guy starting to move a little. He was grunting too, but nothing coherent. Anna looked at the dead guy and noticed he had a large hunting knife strapped to his thigh, just the way Rob and Jack had. Anna unbuckled this and slipped it free.

She removed the knife from its sheath and held it up in front of her face. *Wow, this is impressive.* It was like a Rambo knife, one side sharpened and the other serrated. She used it to release her wrists from the black straps, feeling her skin burning when the plastic pulled away.

Lowering the knife, she allowed the driver to come into view again. He had begun squirming more in his seat but was held up in the air by his seat belt. Anna had no intention of freeing him.

Instead, she directed the tip of the knife towards his thigh before pushing it slowly into his flesh. He grunted out in pain but couldn't speak. Anna had done a good job on his airway with those tie wraps.

She pulled the knife back out, allowing the blood to flow.

Can I be a person who tortures someone else? Although the anger and hatred for these men were still coursing through her, she didn't have the stomach to do much more harm. The only thing she could do now was rid the world of this horrific human being. *Isn't that enough?*

It is enough, and I have to do the ridding. Feeling nothing at having to kill an evil person was one thing, but enjoying inflicting pain on them was another thing entirely. People like these would always exist, but she wasn't going to be one to believe most were good anymore. *I will do whatever it takes to keep the people I care about safe from now on, but there's a line that has to be walked.*

Anna nodded to herself, then pulled the knife across his throat. She had never believed she would be capable of taking another person's life, but now she had—and was 100 per cent justified in doing so. The blood flowed away from his fatal wound and slipped the full length of Anna's left arm, coating her jacket sleeve and hand. She watched it empty out of him, trickling onto what was now the floor of the vehicle. It also covered his dead friend, running over his lifeless face. *Good fucking riddance.*

Anna exited the vehicle via the back doors; it was an effort to open them, but she eventually did. Heavy rain was still coming down, but Anna held her face up to the very English sky and allowed the water to wash everything away. Her fears, her sins, any blood that had splattered her, as well as her remaining tears. She vowed in that moment that they would be the last tears she would cry. *No more.*

Anna retrieved her backpack and crowbar from the vehicle's front section by smashing the rest of the windscreen in. It didn't take much with a tree sticking out of it. She bandaged

237

her wrists, strapped her new blade to her thigh, and positioned her rucksack on her back once more. She then climbed out of the ditch, onto the road before reaching for the locket.

It wasn't there! Anna's hand raced around her chest, searching for the lost piece of silver; it was nowhere to be found. She sighed, then looked ahead at the road she needed to travel down. Her children were that way, not inside the stupid locket. Yes, the metal had soothed her in her most harrowing moments, but she was no longer the same woman who had woken up in a world full of the walking dead. She realised that the only thing she needed to keep her going now was her own mind and the strength she held within it. She wouldn't be stopping herself anymore; she would learn how to fight everything better and harder.

The rain started to slow as she looked back at the van on its side. *I did that!* Anna straightened her spine, turned to face the direction she needed to go, and began hobbling down it.

Chapter 28

Anna wasn't sure where she had left the van exactly, but she walked in the opposite direction that they had travelled. It soon became apparent they were near Burton Pidsea, around six miles from Preston by road but more like five miles cross country.

It took Anna approximately three hours to walk that distance with her slight limp, without seeing a soul on the journey—or a zombie, for that matter. She had skirted around the small villages that cropped up, choosing to take the cross-country trek rather than the road. She didn't have it in her to run into any more people, good or bad.

The blackened clouds had cleared somewhat, and the sun was shining once more. Anna held her face to the warming sunshine, soaking up its rays and allowed it to fill her with positivity. *My kids will be there safe and sound, and Jack and Rob will be fine too.* Anna closed her eyes against the rays. *Please! Please! Please!*

The crows were noisy, and the breeze blew through her hair as she crossed what she hoped would be the final field. She looked down at herself, noticing how much shit covered her clothes and boots. She looked like she had bathed in mud, blood, and gore. *God knows what my hair and face look like too.*

The noise from the birds seemed to get rowdier and then Anna realised why. The unmistakable sound of vehicles on the roads carried on the breeze. Anna's head whipped round to find the source, wondering what the hell she had to face next.

She sprinted to the nearest hedgerow to take cover when a fleet of vehicles came into view: green, armoured vehicles, along with jeeps and covered over trucks. Anna's eyes bulged from their sockets, realising they were here to help. Trucks full of soldiers and armoured vehicles were arriving in their area. *Does this mean it'll all be over soon?*

Anna was about to step out and let herself be seen before Rob's warning spun through her head. Her recent experiences also wormed their way in, so Anna thought better of letting them know she was there. *Just in case.*

They disappeared out of sight before Anna stepped out again. Nothing had changed in her opinion; she still needed to get to her ex-in-laws' place. If the UK got this shit under control, then great, but right now, she was solely focused on getting to her children.

Anna emerged onto the tarmac just down the road from Jill and Ben's. She closed her eyes, wondering what the hell she would see as she approached. *Please let Rob and Jack be ok.*

She reached the spot she had been abducted from and turned a full 360-degrees. She ran between the ditches on both sides of the road but could see no sign of Jack or Rob. *Is this good or bad?*

She tried to make out any markings that may have been left on the road or in the ditch, but she could see nothing. She clambered back out of the gutter and saw two zombies heading up the road from Preston village traffic light section. *Two zombies! No, please, no!*

Anna shuck off her rucksack, pulled the crowbar clear and moved towards them as fast as her sore ankle would allow. They ran straight for her, with the first reaching Anna three metres before the second. It allowed her to distinguish that this one was neither Jack nor Rob.

She cracked its skull open with ease before the second had quite reached her. She brought the crowbar up through the second beast's jaw, holding it up for a moment, looking at its face. She blew out the breath she had been holding and released the beast to the ground. They both had been teenagers, but neither were the people she cared for.

Anna leant down to wipe off her weapon and turned back to get her rucksack, shouldering it across just one side. As she strode the last few steps and neared the driveway, she saw the Toyota Corolla parked there.

Anna's eyes went wide with pure joy, and she rested her palms against the bonnet. She shot to the vehicle's back windows, assessing the interior for any signs of blood or damage. *Nothing!* It looked perfect. She moved around to the front, seeing its cracked windscreen and some blood smeared across it, but it looked superficial. Nothing had got inside.

Anna checked the intercom noticing it was broken. *I guess I've gotta climb it.* She mounted the car bonnet, threw her rucksack and crowbar over the gate, and scrambled over the top. She dropped down, cringing from her ankle striking the ground, but she never let that stop her from hurrying straight up the winding driveway and heading for the front door.

Please, please, please, please, please.

Her new tune echoed through her brain as she tried the door, finding it locked. She banged on it before running around the side and thumping on the glass windows there. She peered through, holding her hands around her face and could see movement inside.

Hearing the front door open, she returned to see the barrel of a shotgun pushing through the gap and a greying mop of hair atop an elderly face.

"Ben!"

"Anna! We thought…" Ben didn't finish his sentence; it seemed he couldn't find the words. He lowered his weapon, looking at it like it was a silly thing for pointing itself at her.

"Ben, my kids? Are they here? Are they ok?"

"Yes, yes, Anna. They are; they're all here. Steve, Alex, Jasper, and Logan." His eyes were glassy as he said all the names she wanted to hear.

Anna began to sob and collapsed to her knees on the tiled porch. She raised her hands to her face, covering her eyes and allowed the tears to flow. Happy tears; these ones were allowed. She couldn't believe it; she had done what she said she would. Her children were here safe, and she had got here too.

"ANNA!"

Anna looked up from her crouched position on the floor to see Steve standing before her. He pulled her up and locked her in a tight embrace, where she continued her now hysterical crying into his shoulder.

"You absolute fucking legend, Anna… Batshit crazy, but unbelievable too," said Steve, still holding her. A few more moments passed before Steve pulled back and said, "You had better come in; there are some people here who want to see you."

Anna sobbed a little laugh out and followed him inside. "Oh, my rucksack, it's near the gate; there are more meds for Alex, as well as other stuff."

"I'll go get it soon, don't worry about all of that now," replied Steve.

Anna nodded an exhausted reply as she was led into the large open-plan kitchen. Her children, Alex and Jasper, ran at her and locked on tightly to her legs and waist. Anna shrunk down to their level and returned the squeezing.

When she opened her eyes, she saw Jill and Ben watching her with tears in their eyes and Logan standing next to them. Anna opened her arms towards Logan and said, "Logan, come here."

Logan ran to her and joined the three of them in the hug-fest. Anna kissed the top of his head before looking him in the eyes and saying, "Thank you so much for helping these guys get here. I knew you were a strong little boy."

Logan smiled, warming Anna's heart even more than she thought possible right now. They were safe, and between them all, Steve, Jack, Rob, and herself, they had made it happen.

"Mummy, you've got blood on your head," said Alex.

"I'm fine, Alex. Especially now I'm with you."

Anna released the children and stood back up, swaying a little, light-headedness washing over her.

"Come on, that's not everyone," said Steve.

Anna's head snapped around to face Steve, and she blinked several times in quick succession. *What is he talking about?*

"Are you coming or not?" asked Steve.

"But… who?"

"Just come with me," replied Steve with a grin on his face.

Anna stumbled behind him as he left the room and began

climbing the sweeping staircase of this beautiful home. He led her towards the first bedroom that they came to and knocked on the door.

Anna was utterly bewildered and couldn't manage a single word until she knew what was going on?

"Come in," said a muffled male voice.

Steve opened the heavy wooden door and gestured for Anna to enter. Anna wasted no time in storming the room; she needed to know who was in there.

She entered, seeing the bright sunshine streaming in through the single pane sash windows, casting sunbeams all over the bed containing the male who had spoken. Anna's mouth dropped open, realising she was looking at the teenage, lanky frame of Jack. He was sat up in the large four-poster bed, with bandages strapped around his midsection and nasty swelling spreading from his nose to his eyes.

"Anna!" Jack looked her up and down. "I… I… Is it really you? Oh my God." He shook his head from side to side. "How did you get here… What happened? You look like shit."

Anna chuckled at Jack's complete shock and his appraisal of her appearance. "I got away… and they won't be bothering us anymore." Anna sobered saying those words. "Rob… Is he…?"

"He's fine, Anna; he's in the next room," Steve cut in, holding up his hands placatingly.

Anna melted onto the bed next to Jack. Everyone was ok. How was this even possible? She turned to Jack and held his hand in both of hers. She wanted to hug him but didn't want to hurt the poor lad more than he already was.

"Oh, Jack, I'm so happy you're both ok." Tears flooded Anna's eyes once more. "Holy crap, I cannot stop crying today."

Jack and Steve both laughed before Steve said, "Rob is in the room opposite; I'm sure he'll be happy to see you if he's awake. I'll leave you to it, Anna."

Anna nodded before turning back to Jack and smiling.

"Anna, go see Rob… like, now." Jack grinned. "Even if he's asleep, wake him up; he'll want to know that you're ok."

Anna smiled at the boy in front of her, knowing the kind of man he was already turning into. His mum would be so proud. She left Jack's room and opened Rob's door, seeing him asleep in the double bed. His left arm and right leg were bandaged with splints, and his head was wrapped above his eyes. Anna hoped there would be no lasting damage.

She sat on the edge of the bed, taking care not to wake him just yet. He needed the rest to heal, and she would wait right here until he awoke. Her eyes roamed over his broken body, and she wished she could lay down next to him. This man in front of her had made it all happen. Between him and his brother, they had saved her and her children's lives many times over.

Anna smiled to herself. *You did it too, Anna. You came through for your children. You learnt how to fight, and you never once stopped until you got here.*

Jack had been right; they were a team and hopefully always would be. No matter what else was to come.

Chapter 29

When Rob awakened, he almost injured himself trying to take hold of Anna. She had had to calm him down and make him relax. His head injury could be a cause for concern, but his fractured limbs needed him to remain immobile for quite a while to come. Of course, no one was sure of the full extent of his injuries. However, they erred on the side of caution and maintained he had to rest. It didn't take him long before he tired and needed to sleep again.

Anna took her leave and found herself in the large bathroom with a hot bath awaiting her, courtesy of Jill. She sat on the toilet seat, taking in her plush surroundings, and processed the last couple of days. *Was that all it was, a couple of days?*

The roll-top tub steamed away in front of her, beckoning her bone-weary body. The thought of hot bubbly water was heaven and seemed too far away just now. The scent of the bubble bath wafted over to her, some kind of lavender, she believed.

She was sitting on the toilet seat, knowing she had to undress but wasn't sure she had any strength left to do it. She had a cut to her head that Jill had wanted to tend to, but Anna had shooed her away, wanting some time alone and to get cleaned up. Sunlight still shone through the windows, with no more signs of dark clouds. Anna breathed in more of the delicious bubble bath and tried to calm her racing mind.

Pain soared through every inch of her body. Her ankle throbbed, but she believed it was only a sprain. What was the acronym? R.I.C.E.? She would get to that soon enough. Her head did hurt, and she intended to look in the mirror soon. Her arms, chest, shoulders, and upper back throbbed with overuse. All that pounding of zombie skulls had taken its toll. And her wrists were cut to shreds but still resided beneath the bandages.

The time had come to take a look in the mirror. She had already taken her boots off, and her feet had been giving off an awful smell ever since. Musty yet very definitely a foot smell. She peeled off her socks, seeing several blisters on both feet, then bent forwards, pulling off her tight-fitted jeans.

It was a battle that revealed many purple patches spread across her legs as well as patches of burnt skin. Anna winced as she pulled the jeans away from her burnt flesh and over her now swelling ankle. Red, purple, and blue covered her, and Anna could feel every one of the bruises as she ran her hands over them. She could hear the stubble on her legs, too, something she might have to get used to if the world was going to carry on going to shit.

Her eyes were heavy, but the bath called to her; she needed to remove the grime and, more importantly, the blood. So much blood had been shed, and she was sure every single moment she had been through added to the amount that now covered her body and clothes.

She pulled her long-sleeved top and vest over her head,

leaving her in just a bra and knickers, and dropped her things on the floor. She stood in front of the full-length mirror and viewed herself for the first time in two days. There was dried blood down the side of her face as well as some bruising spreading out from her cheek, just under her eye. It wasn't just the blood and bruises that shocked her, though; it was everything she was now looking at. She wasn't Anna, works in a bank and has two kids, anymore; she was someone entirely different.

Who? She didn't know. She just knew that she was no longer the old Anna.

She moved her disgusting clothes to the side, and something metallic clattered across the tiled floor. Raking through the clothes, she found her locket—the silver locket she had thought lost in the van crash. She held it in front of her face by the chain, allowing the light to reflect off its shiny surface as it twirled. She didn't feel the need to touch the smooth metal or open it up to see her parents and her children. She didn't *need* it anymore, full stop.

Anna looked back at her reflection and decided that she wouldn't wear it anymore. It was now a reminder of everything she couldn't do, of all the ways she would falter and not have the courage or strength of mind to push forwards on her own. She would keep it because it still meant the world to her, but it was no longer who she was.

Anna moved her body around, letting the pain in, relishing the aches and enjoying everything they provoked. She could kill the dead, and she had killed the living. Neither was particularly enjoyable, but there was a certain kind of satisfaction from having done both. She would not be losing any sleep over the things she had done, and she knew, should the time arise for her to kill again, she would do it in a heartbeat. No remorse.

Anna slid her damaged body into the heavenly bath and smiled, thinking of the fantastic people she had around her. People she would always fight for. She thought of Marcus at that moment and prayed to God he was safe somewhere. Maybe, one day, she would find out what had happened to him.

Her thoughts turned to her daughter and the medication she needed, because they only had a few months of the stuff. *That could be a problem,* Anna thought. But, when she needed to, she would go back out there to find her some more. *That's a problem for a few weeks down the road, though.*

She closed her eyes and allowed the water to envelop her whole body. For today, at least, she would rest and not think about the outside world. But tomorrow, she would plan. There was the Army to think about, and who knew what else was going on out there right now. They had to become more informed, because who knew what tomorrow would bring.

And with a hum and a click, the power cut out.

To be continued...

About the Author

I'm an 80's born Mum of two who loves books more than anything else. I read all Genre's but I write horror because it's what crawls inside my brain and have read it since I was young.

Zombie apocalypse has become my favourite, so much so that I had a story screaming it's way out of my mind. RUN FROM THE DEAD was then created.

I was born and raised in Kingston Upon Hull, Yorkshire, UK. I'm a Yorkshire woman at heart and even decided to set my debut series there too.

I really hope you enjoyed this book. Thank you very much for taking the time to read it.

If you would like to stay informed about my news as well as anything and everything I will be producing, then please visit my website for full details.

Also feel free to contact me on my Facebook page, Twitter and Instagram (all details on the website), as I would love to hear from you. If you want to sign up to my newsletter then please find the info on my website as well.

If you did like this book then please pass on its details to others who you think would love to read it also. Thank you in advance to anyone who does. And keep looking out for more books in the series.

You can connect with me on:

🌐 https://joannenundy.co.uk

Also by Joanne Nundy

Book 2 of the zombie apocalypse series Run from the Dead!

RUN FROM THE DEAD: BOOK 2

When the dead come running, which way do you turn?

Blood flows in the streets as the undead tear limbs and flesh from the living in the city of Hull. A viral rage is unleashed, hitting the UK faster than it can be contained.

On the brink of losing everything, Marcus runs through the housing estates now occupied by the rising dead. He searches for his family whilst learning how to fight the flesh hungry beasts, collecting lost souls along the way.

Christina, a single nurse, hopes her unborn child stays inside her until this madness can be dealt with. Forming new alliances can bring surprises in many forms, proving the world can be shocking for even the most hardened of people. A zombie apocalypse isn't the only thing that can take you by surprise.

The cruel times now thrust upon those still living separate the good from the bad. Some can be trusted with your life and others cannot.

But in a world where the dead have risen, can anyone survive this unchanged?

Printed in Great Britain
by Amazon